Lizard Life

Simone Nobili

To my wife and my two daughters, the cosmic rays in my universe. And to my parents, who gave me life sometime during eternity.

He who makes a beast of himself gets rid of the pain of being a man. —
Samuel Johnson

Introitus

My name is Benjamin Rebujio. I am 50 years old, inching towards 51 with inflamed joints. I was born in New Rochelle, New York, on Locust Avenue, near the Baptist Church. My father was a pharmacist. My mother was a literature teacher. I wore shorts until 7th grade. High school was a blur and a red marker. The day I moved to San Diego to study biochemistry at UCSD, I left with two handbags and no check-in luggage. In 2001, I enrolled in a Ph.D. program in Neuroscience. I began working as a cell biologist in the lab of Dr. Jay Gong. After that, there were three startups in five years where I worked as an operational manager. Then I landed a job at The Nautilus, a company focused on cell-cultured seafood. I became a partner. We made sushi from fish cells, bluefin tuna. When I met Loretta Almazan, she was working as an optometry assistant at Revival Eyewear in 4S Ranch, North of downtown San Diego. She asked me if I was a software engineer. I said no, and why? She said all software engineers take too long to determine if the left eye sees better than the right one. "Can you read the last line for me? Is it an A or an E?" We fell in love, and then we had Reto. It happened in the stretch of a sentence, with just one comma in between. Reto was that comma. Life continued to happen, and what came after was something I could never have imagined. I've danced with chaos and made all the wrong moves. That's when I grew a tail.

Part One

I

It began with a tablecloth drifting over our dinner, turning into the centerpiece of our lives until it faded into a farewell. Our exit from the human race wasn't accidental. We had orchestrated our escape to this very moment, the one that found us gliding down the lanes of the 5 South. I had controlled everything, until I could no longer control anything. As we approached 21 miles from the border, I counted my fingers on the steering wheel, reassuring myself that the human gene was still imprisoned within. I recall the sun dicing my wife's lips into cubes of skin, the moccasin's lining creasing around my sock, my son Reto in the rearview mirror, a spire of sunlight traversing his head. I pulled down the window, and the freeway assaulted my ears. The wind rushed in as whispers, then swelled into a bubbling mouth. As the tires rolled down the freeway, guilt lifted off my chest, only to splatter across the windshield. With each mile closer to the Mexican border, our escape became more tangible. In my mind's eye, I saw us already transformed into lizards, sprawled across the backyard of our San Diego home. That vision became my rosary, each bead a prayer. A grain of sand settled on my thumb. It became a fixation.

***

Our car came to a halt a few inches from the knees of a border patrol agent. I stared at his legs, the uniform draping his limbs like a curtain. The sun reflected the blue of his pants, a layer of asphalt embedded with crushed glass. When I raised my eyes to meet his, my hand opened, presenting three passports. I brought them to the forefront of the scene, offering them up to his scrutiny. The officer's eyes embarked on a journey around each document, inspecting dates, years of birth, last and middle names. I awaited the question, rehearsing the answer, until a lie placed him in the back of my head. I sensed the anatomy of a lizard imprinted upon me, a hologram overlaying my body. It became an act of freedom. While I dissected my thoughts with the machete of logic, Loretta traversed a field of emotions. The sun broke through electric cables. Faces carried voices through market stalls, bullets of sound penetrating gutters, sidewalks, hills and roundabouts. We pressed on toward Geno Sculpt, the med-tech company that pledged reptilian metamorphosis. As my hands glided over the steering wheel, I urged them to grip it tighter, to hold onto the feeling of being human one last time. Fragments of my son's face flickered in and out of the rearview mirror: a sliver of eyes, a piece of mouth, a chunk of brow. Each glance stacked a new piece of the future onto the present. When a red light brought us to a halt, I drifted into a glance toward my wife, assuming that she could feel the echo of my thoughts. She remained wrapped in her own universe. Tijuana felt like a word made for transition, a name that bridged one point to the next with its syllables of suede. The city seeped into my veins, reaching my lungs, flowing down my legs, navigating the interconnected tissues. It gripped my bones and twisted my forearms.

∗∗∗

Nestled inside the cocoon on the road, my eyes traveled to a man, a father bearing two school backpacks. His little girls moved unburdened, heads tilted toward the sky, their feet matching the city's rhythm. The man walked slightly ahead, a folded smile on his face, his shoulders squared under the weight of the bags. I watched him cross the street, feeling like an interloper in his world. I made a passage from my life to his, from a father living in the moment to one stepping out of the human race. The way the man carried the girls' load spoke of commitment to fatherhood, each step scattered seeds of care I had yet to give my son. Every so often, he'd look back at the girls, his head turning like the bow of a ship to witness the depth of his love, before facing forward again. I made up a dialogue between him and his daughters, lending him my own words, a language that could mend every misunderstanding my son and I had endured. It felt as though destiny had arranged this encounter. He became the man I wished I had been, embodying what I had lost but never found. The last thing to fade were the girls' backpacks.

II

Geno Sculpt emerged like a sanctuary of rebirth, where the blades of reincarnation slied through bone and sinew. My gut emitted utterances, a blend of fear and joy. I turned off the car's engine and beckoned Loretta and Reto, their silhouettes etched on the windows. The remnants of our past filled our intestines. Before stepping out of the car, Loretta scribbled a note and left it on the dashboard above the glove compartment. A message tethered to our family name—a square of pragmatism nestled within a circle of madness. They were the final words our lives had written, left for the one who would tow our vehicle, pulling away the last traces of us, erasing what had once been a family, a nucleus of hearts, a failed organism that had belonged to the human race.

***

Geno Sculpt's doors yawned open. A kebab piece of destiny was cut and tossed. Reto followed the trail of my existence walking his own chapter, and so did Loretta. Dr. Camo, a middle-aged man, shuffled towards us extending the fabric of a welcome. His eyes were two brothers cohabiting beneath the roof of a nose. With hands smaller than his arm's length and pecs sagging towards the stomach, he embodied the flawed geometry of a man's body. A desire to skip introductions ripped through the air, but the man handed me a pile of documents before my rush could speak. Then he gestured towards three white chairs, inviting us to fill out the paperwork.

A pen, cold at the base and topped with an eraser button, met my index finger and my thumb. Dr. Camo's palm opened and erupted into a cluster of blue and purple pills. A tone and a voice that nullified emotions explained properties and functions. Though the words escaped me, the pills' colors baited my attention. Dr. Camo repeated himself. *The purple initiates the transformation sequence by interacting with your DNA, while the blue synchronizes with environmental conditions. The combined effects of nanobots and temperature modulation prepare your body for the metamorphosis.* The pills rested in my hands, oval-shaped flags heralding change. I pressed my tongue against the palate, trying to imprint the sight of them on the roof of my mouth. A door creaked open. A nurse with a bobbed haircut emerged, carrying three glasses of electrolyte water, as the label declared. The levels in each glass measured identical to the split millimeter. The tray reflected our faces as the nurse approached, bathed in green light. Each of us took a glass, a communion of sorts, poised to swallow the beginning of the end. I compressed my son into a hug and reassured him that dad would never do anything to harm you. Loretta nodded, her head motion stretching across the frames of her life. I sat beside her, gripping the pen like a protest sign for a world that had let us down. Her fake eyelashes came loose halfway. The sound of pills being swallowed, accompanied by the symphony of droplets of saliva, precipitated onto my ears.

***

The shadow of Dr. Camo came with a filter of detachment. He reached out, his arm crossing into my space, just as I was about to sign the last document. I handed back the pen, painting my lips with my tongue. He led us into a room where OLED monitors covered every wall. Dim lighting, red shadows. The screens assembled a panorama of outer space. I felt pulled inward, my mind lulled into a trance-like state. Reto looked dazed, his face carved into marble. Loretta was focused, locked inside a cell of clarity. Her resolve mirrored my own. The pills had begun their work, igniting battles of heat and cold. Beads of sweat congregated on my brow. Fists clenched, and jaw tightened. My body temperature swayed in a storm of degrees. While Reto let out a cry, Loretta absorbed fear. Reptilian noise in our ears: clicks, chirps, rustles. Our hearing attuned to foreign frequencies. The noise morphed into visual impressions. Unspoken words frozen in time. Hollow, hollow. Dr. Camo became the anchor at the bottom of my ocean. I slipped toward instincts. My perception of space shifted, the room's length stretched, the walls narrowed, and the ceiling rose by a few inches. Texture became vivid, colors hyper-real, senses heightened. Then came the physical surge, agility beyond limits. I moved as if in a trance, speed merging with strength. The room's barrenness wasn't accidental. Between periods of muscle tension, a crawling impulse shaped. My peripheral vision ballooned. I found myself on the floor. Words felt inadequate. We all crawled, still in human form. My limbs throbbed.

III

Chamber One was the Thermogenesis Chamber. Inside, temperature manipulation acted as a biological switch, stimulating cellular change. *Thermosensitive proteins respond to heat or cold, triggering shifts in gene expression, protein synthesis, and metabolic pathways.* I had absorbed fragments of information to soothe anxiety. I had learned that *heat accelerated enzyme activity, speeding up cellular turnover and catalyzing the synthesis of collagen and elastin.* Dr. Camo spoke of the importance of shock response, his words suspended from the ceiling, his voice a knife plunging into a melon. My gaze settled on Reto's arms. His skin had started to change. Color, texture, and thickness no longer felt familiar. His transformation seemed a pace ahead of mine and Loretta's. It wasn't quite lizard skin yet, but something alien was taking hold. I struggled to follow Dr. Camo's instructions. My mind muddled by a haze of comprehension. The cadence of his voice felt like drip from a gutter. His words were obtuse, threaded through the eye of a needle, forcing me to reach for its meaning. His sentences were laced oddly. We stood in front of a hologram projecting the controls of a computer dashboard. At the center was a platform, surrounded by three monitors awash with diagrams. Dr. Camo lifted his hand and issued a set of commands. He directed us onto the platform, where we lay down as instructed. I turned to Reto, feeling the weight of fatherhood, then toward Loretta, grasping for a memory of our shared life. Silence was bloated with fear. The chamber's temperature climbed, hundreds of fires seeping into our bodies. The heat softened our muscles, loosening the fibers. It was a biological reversal: inches disappeared, bones diminished, shapes receded. We thinned into echoes, splinters of what we had once been. The process of slipping away from the human race had been initiated.

***

The pills we had swallowed had scrambled our ability to speak, replacing language with hisses. I'd read about lizards using chemical signals to communicate, conveying messages through particles. While I had understood this in theory, experiencing it firsthand was surreal. I was stupefied to witness my twelve-year-old son being drawn into a genetic shift. As a father, I had failed to forge a connection with him. My focus had strayed, consumed instead by my work. Along the way, I had allowed Reto to fade from my priorities, his presence slipping from my sight. Now, I found myself mourning him while six air vents pushed out nitrous oxide to gift us with euphoria. Despite my resentment toward mankind, memories clung to me like the last ember in a dying fire, sparking a pang of doubt. I ceased to exist the only way I knew how. We had crossed a line where DNA and cellular structures were forever altered. Panic gripped me as my attempts to communicate with Loretta and Reto disintegrated into a series of hissed sounds. I realized my own face, my flesh, everything human, was being re-engineered. My perception of time was changing. The past unraveled into emptiness, the future faded into abstraction. The timeline fractured, leaving only an interrupted sequence of instants. Dr. Camo remained the single point of reference. Yet, through my eyes, he appeared flat, a two-dimensional figure warped by the new monocular sight. As my field of vision expanded and depth perception vanished, the slightest change in the environment was a clash in my corneas. Because of it, I realized Dr. Camo's stillness was intentional. Every move was an invitation to chaos, and could have blown us all over, dry leaves caught in a whirl.

***

We were introduced to a robotic hand. It was a five-fingered construct that released a stream of live silkworms. Instinct took over. I darted my tongue, catching the writhing insects with startling precision. Loretta and Reto moved in a synchronized ritual, each silkworm igniting a primal sense of possession. We became a series of raw impulses, progressing from one waypoint to the next, prisoners to signals that dictated our every move. As the need for crawling intensified, each phase felt revelatory, unlocking a deeper layer of instinct. The physical embodiment of our lizard nature continued to unravel what remained of the human gene. The robotic hand persisted in feeding us. The cycle felt infinite, though fatigue eluded us. The raw primitivism began veering into aggression. Every reaction was an impulse. All I had known was severed, discarded. The remnants of human feelings dawdled. My thoughts quieted, passing through a no-fly zone. Dr. Camo was a detached figure, neither judge nor guide, despite his presence being inevitable. His footsteps released a scent that became our guiding cometh. When the robotic hand paused, silence marked the beginning of a new dread. What now?

IV

Chamber 2 was a cylindrical room. Instead of a traditional door, it featured a narrow slit on one side. As we crawled into it, the space felt imposing. The objects within were colossal, prompting us to huddle together. Electrical conduits snaked across the ceiling and floor. Monitors were fixed at regular intervals along the concave walls, identical in their placement. Dr. Camo moved, seizing one of the red cables to center it, dividing the chamber into two halves and marking an action field. A crane-like apparatus descended, its metallic arms branching into three segments, each ending in a cylindrical housing positioned above the central cord. Inside these housings were magnetic syringes. Dr. Camo initiated the controls, maneuvering the crane until the syringes were directly above us. The red cable was a heat conduit, transferring energy particles to our glands. As the syringes punctured our skin, they marked the beginning of a universe being constructed within our organs. I felt tendrils of matter weave through my bloodstream. These were the nanobots.

***

My obsession with molecular transformation took root in the aftermath of our family's financial collapse, sparking a quest for a new form of existence. My college studies in nanotechnology, combined with the initial phases of therapy, shaped my vision of transformation through the lens of reptilian biology. I'd turned to Ideogram, prompting the AI to generate visualizations of our metamorphosis. While some images felt fantastical, a few captured realisms, grounding my plans. Now, in Chamber 2, lying on the bed with magnetic syringes embedded, it felt like an AI prompt brought to life, with us as protagonists in this generative image. There were no mirrors no reflections, only a darkness that was an extension of the tunnel we'd traversed. Observing Reto's transformation, I discerned genetic shifts. His limbs reshaped, molding him into a young lizard with emerging features. Though still tethered to a human scale, his skin radiated, his body stretched slender and sleek, while his head diminished in size. His eyes, bulging from their sockets, grew rounder and larger. The metamorphosis had unraveled my parental bond. He was no longer the son I knew. A fragment of my own timeline pierced the membrane of my mind, leaking information. A drip of dislodged memories. The stream of thoughts persisted, even though my cellular state was already halfway through its reptilian regeneration. Thoughts coursed through, while my body served as a shell, concealing the turmoil inside. It was about Reto. He never questioned the metamorphosis. The allure of a new existence offered him a glimpse into a simpler life, one where he could just be. We spared him the details of the science behind it, yet he exhibited a visceral trust in us, a loyalty that left him mentally ready to abandon the human race. Unlike his peers, Reto had always been evolving on a different trajectory, existing on the fringe. His quietness was dense, not penetrated by others. He had been diagnosed with high-functioning autism. He was often marginalized by those unfamiliar with his bursts of anger. Since birth, he had danced to a rhythm separate from my own. He was my only child, yet my fixation on neuroscience, tangled with my obsessive-compulsive tendencies and mental clutter, left no space for him to ascend the ladder of my attention. I had retreated from the warmth of love, laying the foundation of his solitude. I had never shared mental space with him. Shielded from the anguish of being a kid searching for a place in his father's arms, Reto had learned to endure. The weight of my guilt pressed on me.

***

Another fragment punctured my mind, releasing a stream of memories that kept my inner monologue running parallel to the phases of metamorphosis. This one was about Loretta. She had walked every step with me, tracing footprints, the wife who kept her own door but built an underpass. We'd met at the Optometric Studio Revival Eyewear in 4S Ranch, San Diego. From that moment, our bond was forged among formulas, equations, and my attempts to reshape reality through quantum physics. She stood beside me, drawing resilience from my ego and fueling my ambition. But when my career in neuroscience unraveled amid financial collapse, a tidal wave struck the shores of our familyhood, reducing our savings to phantom figures. Loretta withdrew, reconstructing a lost world within herself, a realm where neither Reto nor I could follow. I was the architect of her ruin, and while she had followed me, expanding my vision toward a reptilian existence, her trust had become a punishment for her allegiance to my folly. Few questions were asked; even fewer answers were sought from me. Desperation seeped beneath our lives, showing as angry red marks across her face. I never dared to ask if those marks were self-inflicted, or a rash born of suppressed anguish. Loretta had a way of piercing my mind, forcing me to redirect the question inward, like a recurved hook snagging its prey. She was the brackets in the equation I kept trying to solve.

***

When the last piece of memory was snatched from my mind, my posture stiffened, and my chest puffed. Reto replicated my moves, showing the instincts of a young male lizard. Animal tendencies emerged, flashes of my former self surfaced. Shards of life flooded my eyes. I relived the terror of being threatened by the people who drained our savings. I saw Reto's face framed by his bedroom window, his eyelashes fluttering like anxious bird wings, feet rushing, mouth splitting open in a tearless cry. I watched Loretta circling the room, humming through the silence. I glimpsed myself, head buried in my hands, hunched over the kitchen table, fingers twisting, knees scraped, eyes fixed on the garage door. Then I was in the backyard, staring at the patio tiles, tracing the fence as the sky shifted. Voices echoed, anger and regret draping over everything. Before the visual cascade ceased, one final scene burned through: me in the office, studying neural patterns. The worn leather sofa sat in the corner, decaying like a rotten tooth, its holes widening, breathing heavy with time.

***

Dr. Camo reentered my field of vision, his measured steps drawing him closer. I watched him bend at the knees and advancing into my face a giant finger. A message appeared in bio-luminescent text embedded into the floor of the Chamber.

Metamorphic Integration Complete
Specimen Generated

We were lizards. Bright blue bellies, spiny and robust from snout to tail, with muscular builds. Our skin was tough, covered in pebbled scales. Our heads angular and broad, jaws lined with sharp, serrated teeth. Reto's eyes were piercing and almond-shaped, a gleaming copper that radiated alertness. Two ridges ran from his brow down to his neck. Loretta's limbs appeared sturdy, her front claws long and slightly curved. Our tails were muscular and whip-like. I looked down at my chest, watching it expand with breaths. My throat pulsed. Dr. Camo rocked me back and forth, coaxing my body into a rhythm that tempered my tension. I watched as his finger moved to Loretta, cutting through the space between us before landing upon her back. She tensed, her tail stiffening, but a second touch reassured her of his harmless intent. Then he shifted to Reto, who remained still, showing neither recoil nor resistance, a sign that the trust mechanism had been set in motion. Movements fragmented into countless frames per second. When Dr. Camo straightened, it was like watching a building rise to its full height. The crackling of his kneecaps was mesmerizing.

***

The air split into a mosaic of scents that mapped themselves across my tongue, now bifurcated, a single shaft dividing into two lines. As my senses absorbed new information, both visual and sensory, a dry thud emerged, morphing into a rustle. I turned to see Loretta flipped onto her back. Her struggle to right herself painted an image of vulnerability. Dr. Camo retreated, leaving Reto and me to confront the sight. His silence became our first lesson in survival, a quiet baptism into the sacrifices, primal instincts, and raw existence inherent to our new lives. Loretta's twisting and writhing body echoed through the chamber like the strained notes of violins. We became spectators to her struggle, her desperate attempts to reclaim balance amplifying the stillness between us. Each convulsion sharpened into spasms, her contractions violent yet deliberate, punctuated by sharp, empty bites. Finally, after a series of thwarted attempts, she managed to flip herself upright. I felt a flicker of empathy, a shadow of relief, a trace of our past lives clinging to our present. Dr. Camo gestured toward a small area where a cylindrical, transparent flute stood. We crawled toward it, not out of submission but as the only means of movement available to us. Once inside the flute, a cascade of electromagnetic waves enveloped us, illuminating the precise locations of the nanobots within our systems. Their projections flared across the walls, a living map of our transformations. Reto and Loretta aligned with me, our heads tilting in synchronized curiosity, slicing through the flute's midline. Dr. Camo's face untied into a smile. He pointed toward the exit, and we followed, gliding down Geno Sculpt's corridors, crawling along the skirting boards. An appetite for slugs bubbled up within me.

V

The transition from human to reptile had caused our reptilian brain to absorb the limbic and neocortex, intensifying the sense of direction. We were equipped with an acute spatial memory, aided by olfactory receptors that mapped our surroundings. The synergy between our acute smell and reactive reptilian brains lends us a thread of hope in returning home. Although our house was a place bearing the wounds of our past, it now promised the dawn of a new life. Becoming lizards had never been a contingency plan. It was a threaded strategy to reclaim what was lost to loan sharks. If our home was no longer ours to inhabit, then the backyard was our new residence. Fueled by resentment toward the human race, I endured the biological shift because of it. It was a cold piece of logic nested into the need to reclaim what had been taken from me. Crossing the Geno Sculpt doorstep marked the start of a new reality, one where space had readjusted. The concrete glistened, slick with raindrops scattered like marbles across the asphalt. We began scouring the ground for slugs, snails, insects—anything to sate our hunger. The last time we had eaten was before we left for Tijuana. Loretta and I advanced with Reto following behind. Our instincts quickened with every inch we gained, spurred on by the trails left by the slugs. As we neared our preys, we launched the attack, unhesitant. Our movements were synchronized. When I cracked the shell of my first snail, the sound echoed across the parking lot. A wave crashing on the shore. Each bite surged through me, a jolt of vitality. I glanced at Reto, whose snout radiated strength tinged with aggression. Gone was the vulnerability of my son. In its place, the fierce instinct of a young reptile emerged, blade-like teeth glinting in the sun. I bit into another slug, shattering the silence of the parking lot once more. Crashing shells, the swell of slick meat, and no other thought intruding, all of this was unfiltered hunger. The snails were defenseless. I wanted nothing more than to devour, reveling in my place atop the food chain. I became a killing machine with a conical head and a flicking tongue.

***

I noticed our rental car still parked where we had left it. We scaled the tires. The rubber treads gripped our bodies. Reaching the top, I slouched across the hood and slid over the windshield. Loretta's gaze landed on the note she'd left before entering Geno Sculpt. A hiss filled the air, drawing my attention. She remained fixed, feet clinging to the windshield. Reto's posture radiated confidence. Unasked questions lingered. I crawled toward Loretta, my eyes locking onto hers. The air between us thickened with recognition, chemistry born of proximity. The note wasn't just a piece of paper. It was an indictment, a relic of our disgrace. Nothing could have saved us from the precipice we had chosen. My investment in cultured-cell fish, once heralded as a breakthrough, stood as a symbol of my hubris. Here we were, reptiles' legs suctioned to a car's windshield, staring at what once was. The past felt fragmented, a tense in a vocabulary littered with caskets at every word. The metamorphosis had drained the pulp of our emotions and rewoven it. A doubt settled somewhere in my chest. What was I feeling? I noticed my tail, its own movement crossing Loretta's body, developing into a gesture of contact, a piece of sorrow wedged between us, stuck in the teeth of our pain. She must have known that we both remembered, that once we were human, and that we had the audacity to rewrite life's algorithm. We stayed on that windshield for ambiguous pieces of time, all stitched together, while Reto had already descended, hunting a couple of slugs that had escaped the chase. Life was so extreme in the reptile world. If I still had fingers, I would have grabbed it and watched it dangle.

VI

The banks of the Tijuana River showed no mercy, the winds tearing at us like demons. Branches, rocks, shrubs, and mud blurred into a single dimension. Our tongues cut through the air, searching for the path to San Diego. Leaving behind the sterile confines of Geno Sculpt, we perforated the wilderness. We hastened along the northern bank. A thread of instinct bound us together. In survival, we moved as one. A flock of ducks watched us crawl, tilting their heads. It was a choreographed dance. This marked first moment another species acknowledged us as lizards. The snails we had consumed were prey, their existence peripheral to ours. But the ducks were aware of our presence. Reto stared back at them. Loretta glanced over them. I remained still, captivated by the ducks' rounded chests. One among them broke from the flock and approached. It felt as though a mirror had been placed between us, each observing with mutual interest, scrutinizing our physical differences, adjusting to the uncommon sight. A few pieces of time rolled by, then the wind's mouth grew loud. A soft quack from the duck stamped our safe passage. As we prepared to traverse Otay Mountain, we found respite near a shrub, waiting for the sun to break through the clouds. When it finally emerged, our bodies came alive. The warmth seeped into our veins, flowing in rhythm with our breathing. We absorbed every ray, stretching limbs and tails. Squinting to soften the glare, we indulged. Our skin began to shift in color, each scale humming with regenerative power, operating with minute precision. A defense mechanism. Patterns formed and dissolved, reassembling like soldiers in a parade, marching in rectilinear motion before breaking into clamorous pivots. I lingered in the warmth, letting fragments of peace blend with fear. In silence, I wove a fabric of intents, committing to endure the journey. A silhouette broke into view.

***

A pelican's flapping wings kicked up a swirl of mud, raining dirt upon us. Reto pivoted into a defensive stance while Loretta and I braced for the threat. Flattening ourselves to the ground, we surged forward. The pelican's wings beat with fury, narrowing in on Reto with a cacophony that echoed down the riverbank. We blended into the mud and slipped into the hollow of a sycamore tree. Inside the trunk, our tails tangled. The space was cramped for three lizards, but there was comfort in that closeness. Outside, the bird's wingbeats mauled the face of the air. We stayed motionless, holding our breath, claiming the tree's damp, until the sound of the wings receded into the distance, merging with the murmur of a water stream. The thick scent of decay. Fungi clung to the tree walls, beetles scurried, each absorbed in their own cycles of survival. Hunger struck, quick and sharp. The swing of an axe. I lashed out with my tongue, snapping up a line of ants in a single movement, my eyes locked on the pelican's shadow. My tongue flicked again, a flash of pink in the dim light, pulling most of the ants into a cluster of death. The sound reverberated as my throat absorbed the catch. One ant carried on, oblivious to the disruption in its ranks. Stillness once more, frozen limbs, molded by fear. Silence compressed into a pocket signaled the pelican's departure. I turned to Loretta. Relief had found home in her gaze. I remained tense.

Residual terror. Fragments of my instincts fused with Reto's. His distress pulsed through the tail, then curled over my head. A memory of him being bullied at school resurfaced. It gushed out, I should say. The schoolyard; cement, voices, jackets, shoes, feet, faces. Blood from a broken nose. Reto, thrown to the ground, kicked in the stomach, slapped on the back of his head, whipped with an iPhone cord. His pain carries the sound of a clogged sink, hair twisting, stuck in the drain. When he comes home, we bath him. We clean him. We do nothing else. No charges are pressed. No protests are made. We hide.

***

Reto's tail unfurled, his body tensed, anger and impatience. He sprang from the hollow, eyes fixed eastward. He moved with purpose, as if his claws had brushed against an electric wire. Fear was the final pin to dislodge. His urgency quickened my own movements. He was now a force, a young reptile shedding his former self. As I crawled, my bifurcated tongue nibbled particles in the air. A triatic of scents: gasoline, rubber, and scorched metal. Then came the sound of an engine, cutting through like fangs. Silhouettes of border patrol agents emerged against the foothills, flat shadows sharpening as the engine's roar grew louder. The patrol car advanced, churning up clouds of dust. We pressed our bellies to the ground, eyes fixed on the threat. The vehicle rumbled past, its wheels carving grooves, air thick with the acrid scent of burnt rubber. As the dust settled, we emerged. Togues flicking, we resumed our crawl toward Otay Mesa. We quickened our pace, hearts racing, towering metal panels of the US border wall. Around their base, tunnels filled with concrete. Reto crawled into one of them, vanishing behind a concrete block. Loretta's eyes tracked along, and I turned to her, gliding through her pupils, wandering across her corneas, seeking reassurance. She wanted me to take control. I jerked my tail to call a line-up before sneaking through one of the openings. Rusted planks. I bobbed my head, a piece of the sky crumbled onto my tongue. I took notice of the sun. I was the hand of a kid in a class full of students after having given the chance to speak. I was the first one to cross the border.

VII

The scent of The Wall. With our backs turned, each inch of distance eroded its presence. Its tang faded from the air, dissolved, a collapse of intensity. We pressed onward, assaulting the mountain's foothills. Fear was a load to carry. Life as animals brought tension, heightened alertness, spikes and spears of survival. It costed us everything. Fatigue never ceased to exist. To endure it was to grow into full reptiles, to accept the hunt and the prey, the game of death, the rules of evolution. But it was our journey and no one else's. We gave it to ourselves, we brought it upon ourselves, we had learned it. You could see it in the way we crawled, the synchronized motion, undulating against the earth, the focal points all in line. My hydrant eyes, from here to there to everywhere. We never lost sight. Death carried us forward. It was the lizard life.

***

A hump broke through the horizon, surrounded by chasms of dust. It closed the gap. It ruptured my crawling rhythm. An intruder breaching my mind, flooding it with a dull cacophony. Reto's courage receded, an ebbing tide. Loretta's muscles tensed, a musky scent laced with ammonia. Her stance unfolded like a rehearsed sequence: tail curled, body flattened, skin aglow. I froze mid-crawl as the noise penetrated the ground, jabbing at our bellies. Six young adult javelina came into view, short legs and dark brown patches streaking their coats. Their protruding canine exuded menace. My eyes dropped to their sharp hooves, poised and braced for action. The squadron pounded the ground, each footfall a war declaration. They tore through the dirt, battering mud and splintering roots. Their grunts erupted in a symphony of dominance. With heads held low and tusks pointed forward, they charged in formation. I slipped into a crevice. When I glanced back, the javelina's eyes were battered by a flurry of punches from the dust. Loretta and Reto had each claimed their own crack in the ground. It was the first time we'd been apart since the metamorphosis. It only took the cradle of an instant for them to vanish, eaten by the earth's mouth. Inside my crevice, I braced. Acute solitude, unlike anything I'd ever known. Pressing my legs against the walls of the crevice, I strained to hoist myself up, desperate for a glimpse of my wife and son. When the ground trembled with the oncoming herd, memories from my past life began to flood.

***

I am sitting at the dinner table. Reto is on my left, Loretta on my right. I stare at the water pitcher while pretending to listen to Reto. I am elsewhere, nowhere, lost in the cell-cultured fish market, juggling investors. A hollow half-smile clings to my face, its edges fraying beneath the surface. A façade crafted to shield my son from my disconnection. Reto's words drift like weightless scraps, vanishing before they can register in my head.

***

One javelina split from the group, stopping inches from my hiding place. Its snout twitched, probing the air and flooding the narrow crevice with its presence. I caught glimpses of its nostrils. Musky scent, hunter and prey. The skunk pig rammed the crevice once more, flaring closer. My thoughts skimmed over Reto. His safety was out of reach, somewhere in the chaos of my mind. Another memory.

***

Dominic Bovisa's breathing is loud. He tries to kick my office door down. Two security guards rush in. He's the loan shark I owe money to. One of the investors at The Nautilus. What have you done? A criminal. I told the board we needed to raise money. Scale up the business, scale up some more. What now? My chest tightens. I press myself against the wall, ears straining. A furnace of loudness. Dominic is a snarling animal just outside my door. I curl tighter into a corner, clutching my knees to my chest. I stay where I am.

***

The javelina's scent gripped my intestines, thick and inescapable. Its snout filled my view, probing deeper into the crevice. I pushed myself further into the darkness, wriggling down through damp, constricting interstices. From below, the pig's nostrils were two black lentils. The noise swelled, muscular, unstoppable, until it reached a crescendo, before diluting into stillness. The javelina relented. It couldn't pry open the crevice. Silence seeped through the foothills of Otay Mountain, mingling with the faint songs of birds.

***

When I ascend the crevice walls, my eyes caught flecks of sky. I scanned for Reto and Loretta. A hiss drew my attention to the left. Turning, I spotted Loretta's head silhouetted against the light. Then, from the right, came a chirping sound. It was

Reto, flicking his tail. Our eyes locked, our breathing shallowed. We moved closer, converging along the dirt path. The sun sagged, a marshmallow roasting over a stick. Cold crept into my bones, threading icy tendrils beneath my claws. We pressed forward, crawling North along the trail toward Camp Minnewawa. We sliced through brush, weaving in and out of the mountain's creases. Our tongues flicked, mapping the road ahead. We climbed slopes, tails brushing against the ground, scattering stones. The terrain was unforgiving, branches tore at our skin, rocks bit into our limbs. Yet each grip felt surer, our bodies adapting to the reptilian life. Fear resolved like a problem worked out to its logical end.

***

We crawled into the remnants of Camp Minnewawa, a WWII bunker fractured into two buildings, a broken tooth in the mountain's gaping mouth. Rusted gates hung crooked, their hinges clinging to the past, graffiti covered the walls, layered in bold, angry scrawls. Around the bunkers' perimeter, charred weeds carried a scent of gasoline. The traces of human passage: torn clothes, empty containers, broken bottles, truncated chains, and the ashen remains of extinguished fires. Our eyes settled on a crack in the far wall, slicing through a graffitied word, *HOPE*. The crack ran deep, wide enough to serve as a hiding place. I scaled the wall, sliding into the fissure between the *O* and the *P*. Reto and Loretta lingered below, their eyes tracking my ascent. When I disappeared into the crevice, they followed. Reto slipped under the *H* while Loretta eased into the space beneath the *E*. We flattened our bodies against the cold, jagged interior. Tails folded tight, breaths slowed to a shallow pace. Together, we adjusted to the cadence of the night.

VIII

A dream surged through a barrier of blackness. At its center, a grid glowed, a green core edged with red-orange tones. Images from the dream filtered through it, loud chunks of life, all from before the metamorphosis. They flickered in and out, the passing sporadic. I could hear a beat. When the first image surfaced, it spread outward. I watched myself speaking before Dominic Bovisa, pitching the cell-cultured fish business as a next-level investment in tech. A single beat thumped. *Dominic's mouth opens, a silent scream spilling out in liquid chrome, dripping over me. The death threats take the shape of a red blade, while the words leaving my mouth are rigid, squared like floor tiles. I have three knives stuck into my skull.* Two more beats echoed, one short and one long. *I stand before The Nautilus board of directors. Rain thumps on tin roofs, water flooding into the office. Four figures loom in front of me. I am submerged, mouths moving in unison. This is the day of my ousting. The word is UNFIT. It's three-dimensional and floats.* Three beats reverberated. *Loretta's face is marred by razor-sharp tears. A trapdoor opens beneath her. She falls into it. Her hands streak across my chest. Her face contorts, reshaping into a cube, each side bearing multiple eyes. Her body disassembles and reassembles in loop. The garage door of our house opens. It's me, honey, it's me. Loretta is holding the phone. My pupils leave the sockets, drawn into the phone's screen. They witness all our bank accounts zeroing out, the numbers disappearing as I watch.* I was yanked from the dream. A switch was flipped. I found myself back in my lizard form. The night had turned colder. Reto lay curled into a tight ball. Loretta had her body flat against the wall, breathing slow. Camp Minnewawa stood unchanged. Everything was exactly as I'd left it before sleep. My muscles eased, but my eyelids grew heavier, denser, opaquer. In the background, the grid flickered back into focus. It started all over again.

***

Two beats reverberated. *Loretta's left leg is severed at the knee, the joint replaced by a marble emblazoned with the number 21. Two lawyers from The Nautilus stand in front of me, urging me to sign a stack of documents. The number 21 glows on their foreheads, and I understand: $21 million is the lawsuit's price tag. My thoughts unravel, each one a thread woven by my own hands. Then our mailbox materializes, twisting into the shape of an octopus. Its tentacles stretch wide, a fish-shaped ornament glaring from above the doorbell's chime. Loretta's skin turns translucent, exposing the rings of her trachea. Her cheekbones jut sharply, the malar bones poking through her skin. In her hand, she clutches the foreclosure notice from the bank.* Three beats sounded, each equal in length. *Reto sits on the black leather sofa, engrossed in the TV. With each spoonful of Cheerios, the drops of milk trigger his chest to rise in heavy breaths. I find myself drawn into his lung. Intercostal muscles. His diaphragm contracts, his ribcage expands, and the echoes of school bullies' voices fill his chest cavity. The bowl of cereal disappears from Reto's hands and reappears inside the TV, a prop in a show. Reto vaporizes. a wet stain left on the sofa.* A sharp beat shattered the air. *A door stands alone in the middle of a landfill, dark brown wood, double locks, glass panels at the top. It's our house door. A man climbs a pile of trash, clutching an eviction notice. His mustache devours his face until nothing remains but a shadow. A harsh noise escapes my lips, blending with the clatter of the landfill. I feel trapped. Around me, a coyote with broken legs limps in circles, a snake lies flattened under a truck's tire, old woman's feet wrapped in varicose veins shuffle towards the kitchen. The pain detonates, shards of fresh plaster against the door. The landfill collapses on itself.*

My eye caps returned to their natural clarity. My eye muscles reengaged, scanning for Reto and Loretta. They were exactly as I had left them. Curled in stillness. A ray of sunlight struck the tip of my tail, its warmth spreading like silicone inside a pipe. The beam reached Reto and Loretta, splitting to nudge them awake. Reto stirred first, his limbs stretching, tail unfurling in slow ripples. Loretta's eyes snapped open, darting around with sharp twists. The sounds of the mountain rose steadily, deep tones ascending into a persistent hum. Exchanging brief, pulsing glances, we crawled down to the base of the wall. Emerging outside the bunker, we claimed a strip of dirt where the sun's rays bore down with full intensity. Flattening ourselves against the ground, we absorbed the heat, poised above the earth. The wind drifted from the mountain foothills, carrying notes of buckwheat and chamise.

IX

A platoon of rays passed through our skin. The sun was doing its work, Reto and Loretta were deep in their thermoregulating process as I was. A pulsating image of a new day throbbed in my mind. From Otay Mountain and into the San Ysidro, a journey awaited. I found hunger before anything else. It struck me and landed into my hormones. It activated the predatory instincts and made energies converge to a single mission: to hunt. I spotted a cluster of centipedes at the bottom of the smaller bunker. The connection between me and them was established by the twitching micro-movements of my pupils, dilated like a yolk thrown into a hot pan. I accelerated the crawl, covering the distance between the two bunkers, down a hill, lubricating moves with no resistance, in a circle of continuum momentum, as if the ground beneath me had lifted and I was surfing on waves of air. My eyes locked onto one of the centipedes, fragmenting the scene into monochromatic figures. My body lowered its balance, muscles coiled like a taut spring, and I was ready to strike. The centipede scuttled along the ground, its many legs moving in rippling motion. I lunged forward and snapped open my jaws. The centipede barely had time to react before it got caught between my teeth. I clamped down, piercing its segmented body. The exoskeleton gave way. The centipede writhed and twisted in a tango of moves. Its legs flailed in a desperate attempt to escape. I readjusted the grip. Through a vicious series of bites, I began devouring the insect, swallowing its entire length at an orderly pace, each bite more efficient than the one before. I was compost in my action, necessary in my need, devoid of any possible waste. The engineering of my bite was so natural that it felt engraved in my master regulator gene. The centipede's struggles faded into anonymous defeat that stung the remnants of its pride. There was no resistance it could oppose that would have spared it from the kill. It was the food chain at work, winding the hollow corridors of my gut. The centipede's body was steadily pushed down from the esophagus to the stomach, where the muscular walls had begun the churning, breaking it into pieces, allowing the gastric juices to ease the work. When I caught the blurry silhouettes of Loretta and Reto springing onto their prey in the net of my eyes, I luxuriated in the feast. Killing spree. The basic needs of my own sustenance contained within a nutshell of actions. The feast lasted just long enough for our circadian rhythm to sync with the heartbeat of satiety. Then, the journey to San Ysidro begun.

***

The wilderness of Otay Mountain was hostile, forcing us to claim every inch and adapt. Jagged rocks, sharp boulders, loose gravel. It was a journey birthed from the womb of nature. A brutal decline sapped our strength, draining endurance from our limbs. Tension filled each step as we climbed back up and pushed through thick clumps of grass. Directions were imprinted in our claws, reactions designed into our muscles, and the physicality of our beings was all wedged into the moment. The more we distanced from the top of Otay, the more the marine layer thickened. The San Diego Bay was immersed in bubble wrap. The mist kept the sun at bay, and the blue of the sky, though about to burst into pieces of cobalt yellow, waited for its time to be ripe. Then the temperature increased, the coolness got hacked. Descending further, the terrain transitioned into chaparral, dense, low-lying shrubs. Brushes appeared everywhere, popping out one after the other. We darted through the vegetation, undulating to fit through the tight spaces between the roots of the sycamore trees. When the mountain scenery evolved into a long strip of coastal sage scrub, the ground softened, revealing patches of soil and pebbles. Our steps grew springier, with our tails serving as stabilizers. The descent into the grasslands reduced the struggle, less work for our claws. Tall grasses and open space welcomed us, we widened the strides, staying low to the ground, eyes sharp and alert, scanning for threats. The wind's electrical fingers pushed from behind.

***

In the grassland, a string of a remote thought unraveled. *I am in my twenties, camping at Clarence Fahnestock, up in New Rochelle. The land beneath my feet, the stance of my youth, the expanse of the sky, it's all a map of possibilities, an everywhere for anywhere. Many years later, I would come to see this as the sole fragment of happiness, crushed by the rusty pliers of nostalgia. Bleeding over the years, I bottled myself in hatred, resenting everyone for the abuses inflicted upon me. But now, in the grasslands, in lizard form, I touch that speck of an instant again. It's my immediate forever.*

***

We traversed the last stretch of open land. The scent shifted, a new palette of odors. Our pace slowed. We lunged at insects. Our throats swelled in synch. Billows of smoke rose ahead, stitching together the outline of the city. The edges of the sky were confined to a narrowing square, clouds accelerated across the horizon. A colossal ball of dirt ascended into the air. Gravel spiraled, my bifurcated tongue flailed, unfamiliar spaces in my mouth. The ball ruptured as a hauling truck blasted through, an angular projectile tearing across the land. Another truck followed, then another, until the choking haze expelled a full convoy. We scrambled into a crevice, retreating into the earth's veins for shelter. Huddled together, our tails entwined, we shared warmth. The fleet rumbled on. The trucks surged forward, engines growling with raw, mechanical fury. A spiral of scent wound its way onto my tongue: diesel, kerosene, gasoline, burnt clutch, charred rubber. The air thickened, laden with rusted fumes. The convoy barreled toward the border, away from our direction, yet their force felt magnetic, pulling me backward. My instincts faltered. A ripple of energy surged through Reto's body. It was a pulse that sank deep into my skull.

***

An opening at my brain's core pulled forth another memory. *Reto steps off the school bus, his face streaked with tears. A seventh grader had called him names in front of everyone, pelting him with chewed candy. Humiliation pools at the corners of Reto's mouth. His lips crack. A miniature version of me falls off his chin. I am a plastic figurine. I am poorly made. I think of my own bully, Dominic Bonvisa, and the helplessness that chains me. I can't even protect myself, let alone anyone else. Reto's feet steps on mine, pinning me in place. My arms are tied. My hands are chopped at the wrist. I walk away, but the weight of sorrow binds us both. Reto dissolves into the fog. The bus disappears with him. A suffocating limbo presses in from all sides.*

***

A truck thundered over the crack above us. The light vanished, eclipsed by rubber tread. Loretta's silence deepened, her eyes widening. The tire pressed down on our pocket of air. It passed over our heads like a needle slipping in and out of a vein. It started dripping oil and raining gravel. The closeness to death reassembled our reptile lives. The scent of burned rubber pressed down on my tongue like a phantom weight. We had slipped past danger, carried forward on a new streak of fate. We emerged into the light once again.

X

The edge of the city revealed itself like a nasal cavity, its nostrils flared ready to be explored. Slimy stomachs. We crawled onward, leaving behind the bloated memory of the hauling trucks, their presence dissolving into relics. Along the way, I began constructing a lab of scents, a collection of odors imprinted in my mind: trees, branches, gravel, shrubs, cement, concrete, steel rods, dried cactus, wilted roses. Loretta and Reto kept a close distance. I imprisoned their silhouettes in my retina. My third eye was a lighthouse. It signaled dangers, piercing through curtains of shades. The more we penetrated the city's intestines, the more my confidence grew. Barriers, tunnels, flyovers, curbs, ramps. I found my claws reactive, my animality unlayered. No glitch in the system, only fluid motion.

***

Beyer Boulevard Trolley Station, perched on a spur of the San Diego Eastern Railway, was the destination my instincts had charted. Our next task was to climb into the exhaust pipes of a bus and ride it to Balboa Park, where we would spend the night. Up in the Otay region, we had not encountered anyone but here in the outskirt of San Ysidro, as soon as we crawled into the streets, we had been forced to deal with the crowd. The most menacing roadblocks were feet, of all kinds, stomping, passing, running, crossing, marching, standing. They brought a whole new set of sounds with them, embroidered in the curtain of air, loud and persistent. I created a cartogram of straight and later movements, to be printed over my instinctive responses. The ground was a mosaic of textures: smooth concrete, treacherous cracks, stray pebbles, sharp turns into busted alleys. Each footfall created a seismic event, sending vibrations through the ground. My eyes darted in all directions. The reflective surfaces from passing vehicles vomited a dizzying array of stimuli. San Ysidro was okra and cobalt blue, orange and opaque white. It was colors that existed in my human genes and were poured on top of my reptilian retina. The sun's face had a long neck, and its yellow fingers reached everywhere. All was lingering there for me. Reminiscence. Senses in overdrive, mind overloaded, limbs overworked. I looked at Reto. He radiated courage. The bobbing of his head carried firmness. His youth landed in waves. Loretta came wrapped in a different demeanor. At times, she seemed to drift, trailing without momentum. The journey had no straight lines. Dodging and pivoting. To know how to reverse path was more crucial than the path itself. The architecture of our sight. It was the epitome of cause and effect, shaping the way forward. To fight with shadows. The towering structures of buildings projected umbra onto the ground like stucco from a trowel. Patches of darkness. The air thickened with fumes from the food trucks, traveling upwards into the pigeons' nares. I found myself following their flight path, a geometric marriage of perpendicular, oblique, and horizontal trajectories. Flocks taking off and landing. Loretta paused over a manhole. She had flattened her body against the grated cover. My mind drifted away from the reptilian universe.

***

A memory reemerged. *Loretta stands off the terrace overlooking our backyard. She's climbed over the railing and leans out. Waves of humming from the 15 freeway saturate the wind. It takes a few seconds for my thoughts to align before I start moving toward her. She leans further into the void, her left hand clenched into a blood-pressured fist around the eviction notice. On my third step forward, she turns, registering my presence, her grip on the railing faltering. I'm already there, catching hold of her. We collapse. She makes a guttural sound. Her insides have been shuffled by the fall. We lie on our backs. Tears cling to her jawline before sliding down to her humerus. She agonizes, and I, helplessly, agonize with her.*

✳✳✳

Loretta was wedged in the manhole's grate, her body caught between the metal bars, struggling to free herself. Guilt swelled inside me, as if I were to blame for everything that had happened to us. Reto had stopped crawling, his eyes locked on his mother. She gave him a nod in return. The moment stretched, stripped bare to its framework. Loretta's tail scribbled arcs in the air, her claws scraping, a jagged symphony that gave pain a voice. I crawled toward her, but my body stiffened as my mind commanded it forward. I felt severed, a defective machine. A spear through the ribs, a private crucifixion. My eyes flicked upward and saw a bicycle hurtling toward the manhole. Loretta freed herself at last, slipping loose in the nick of time. My eyes chased her while anchoring a few disjointed thoughts. She crawled away from the bike. The memory that had pierced me dissolved. An empty pocket in my mind.

✳✳✳

At the bus station, we found ourselves in a new landscape of feet. Pointed boots, square heels, suede, leather, a swarming surface of shoes and sneakers, each like a crater on the moon. With nowhere to hide, we navigated through it all. We moved as one. If I crossed a muddy puddle or skimmed the edge of a sidewalk, Loretta and Reto mirrored me, their movements wired to mine like clockwork. Feet passed by with objects tethered to them. Trolleys, bags, backpacks, their weight bearing down without warning. Reto collided with a suitcase, his tail swinging atop mine to regain balance. Loretta wove through a torrent of wheels, her movements instinctive, a dance of muscle and survival. We devoured the path ahead then crawled to the back of the bus. Slipping beneath the chassis, we sought refuge near the suspension, where nooks and crannies could shelter us once the vehicle was in motion. The tube walls were coated in dark residue, half-burnt fuel, soot, a thick, acrid smell seeping into every breath. Above me, a portion of the sky framed itself in the round mouth of the exhaust, a perfect circle of blue held steady. The scent of scorched fuel and the sharp tang of heated metal fused into a trap of our own making. We held our calm.

***

When the engine roared to life, a symphony of high-pitched metallic notes echoed through the machine's depths. Within moments, heat and fumes surged through the muffler, filling the air with a choking density. We huddled deep within a cranny in the frame, near the suspension. I wedged myself tightly between the rear left tire and the spring. A low clang, followed by a cascade of echoing clicks from the gearbox, heralded the bus's departure. My tongue flickered, my tail twitched. A dusty rattling universe. Thoughts floated, loose marbles in a jar. I strained, forged a mental tether to my family. From the nook near the rear suspension, catching a glimpse of either Loretta or Reto was impossible. Solitude pressed, anger simmered. Jagged bursts. Old wounds refused to quiet.

***

A memory tore through my lizard life. *A call from my lawyer, urging me to sit down and listen. I curl up in a corner. I focus on my feet. The floor is undulating in sync with the lawyer's words. His voice is metallic. He tells me the bank has claimed the house. Foreclosure is final. There's no appeal, no extension. My home isn't mine anymore. Silence clangs in my ears. I glance at the door. Loretta and Reto are on the other side of it. I don't move. I keep listening to the lawyer's voice, sinking. It's all grey and viscous. Pain lubricates my legs, and I slide down onto the floor.*

***

I spotted Reto clinging to the gearbox. My tail twitched. Steadying myself on his pointed head, I traced the ridges between his eyes. The more I focused on him, the more the noise distilled into a hum. Beneath his skin, within the rhythm of his lungs, lay the strength I needed. A bond began to weave itself between us. I shared my guilt with him, tangled with the hatred I'd buried. The moment I turned away, searching for Loretta, half of the bus reassembled itself before my eyes. She emitted a faint hiss. The gearbox shifted with fat clicks. The grueling state returned, enclosing us in a womb of machinery. I turned back to Reto, and with that, the unobserved part of the world blinked out. I shut my eyes. Two fists of blood vessels. To regain control, I resolved to look only at my son for the rest

44

of the journey. I stayed fixed on him, my gaze clamped onto his snout, gripping tight. I didn't let go. My eyes had grown teeth, sinking into Reto for salvation. I fixated on him, drawing out his confidence, draining it to poison the cowardice in me. The disgraceful, vile fear of dying. I locked Loretta out.

***

The bus slowed. Diesel and rubber thickened the air in clusters. My claws unlatched from the tubular frame, a ship leaving its harbor. I hovered above the asphalt, an electric pulse carrying me until I landed flat. Loretta and Reto leapt down beside me. We were three once again, under a sky of mechanical limbs. Shocks, arms, axles, tanks, and lines. Machine trench, ready and arrayed. Beneath the bus, a stream of feet passed in a psychedelic cloud. A low, circular motion surrounded us, reverberating through my ears. Each noise came like a briny wave, delivering sharp, tactile images: rough, layered, and swirling faster whenever I closed my eyes. The images escaped and returned, playing games in my limbic system. It was as though someone had taken control of me, twisting dials, shuffling reactions, amplifying my mind in ways I couldn't command. I didn't know if Reto and Loretta felt the same. Their gazes wrapped around me, carrying unspoken questions.

XI

The air churned with odor, a fog of sensory chaos. I was disoriented. I raised my tail and bobbed my head, drawn by an impulse that slid under my skin. Loretta and Reto pressed close, occupying the same patch of asphalt. I had to find our way home, but I realized we were inside a homeless tent. A jagged tooth in the mouth of the city. I jerked my head, emitting a hiss that vibrated. A man sprawled across the sidewalk, encircled by jars of spoiled food. Each jar encasing misery in fetid stillness. The man's head rested on egg cartons, and his shoes, split down the middle, exposed toes that clawed into the air. A chain encircled his waist, fastened with a padlock to keep his pants secured. The restless toss of his body sent the chain scraping the asphalt. I crawled away from the man's feet, two sunken islands in a sea of cracked concrete. Loretta and Reto broke from their paralysis and fell in line, trailing my path.

***

Crossing the street was a game of high-stakes riddles, each move a gamble against the city's grinding machinery. I faced it head-on, hyperaware of every angle. The asphalt exhaled heat into our bodies. My tongue flicked, mapping an intricate web of scents. Every cracked sidewalk, every shadowed alley was proof of my persistence. Loretta and Reto followed without hesitation, loyal to the path I was carving for them. From time to time, our heads dipped low, hunting for anything that could sustain us. In those moments of primal hunger, my gaze would narrow, locking onto the fattest beetles. I'd spring forward, the sudden motion rasping off the ground beneath me and slicing the air with a sharp, jarring sound. The beetles' shells glinted like sparks escaping a fire, and in a heartbeat, one would be between my teeth. Its legs flailed, a frantic windmill of pain, igniting a surge of adrenaline. The cracking of the exoskeleton was the steady cadence of a drumbeat. Chewing became methodical. The mechanical precision of the jaw. The hunt channeled my need to assert dominance over the prey. To penetrate the flesh was to traverse death. I existed in savagery. Clumps of impulses ran through my body. Whenever the fever of the hunt settled into a state of calm, I would push forward, dragging myself across the dirt. Then something within, a trigger hidden in the hollow of my intestines, would snap again. And I would return, tearing insects and feeding on the notes of their suffering.

***

Emerging from the meandering paths of Balboa Park, we moved toward the Hillcrest neighborhood. The landscape felt alive, a beast in my third eye. We crawled along the street edges, always poised to deflect danger and slip into stealth. Leaping over roots, weaving through underbrush, vaulting fences, gripping ledges, skidding on dust. The horizon sat on the tip of my tongue. I devoured countless bit of life. Repetition bordered on exhaustion. A flatline of primal urgency. There was no pause, no breath to step beyond survival. It was existence at the brink.

***

A foreign sound struck, it landed on my ears like radio disturbance. It rose, fell, clashed, dissolved, and returned, louder each time. A tug-of-war played out by rogue sound waves. Paralysis shattered my muscles. My legs locked. Loretta and Reto hissed. The waves grew, wearing down my nerve endings. My vision dimmed, my limbs blurred. Loretta and Reto circled, their tails nudging me, hisses escalating into cries. I unraveled, my animality dismantled by an unknown force. The sound pierced through me. Time fragmented. I was disintegrating on a patch of asphalt, my claws dissolving, Loretta and Reto fading. There was a hollow arc stitched into that moment, a conductor's baton frozen midair. My focus wavered. The feeling of being steered. No, manipulated. The sound carried weight, a force that pinned me down. It drained me. It hollowed me out from the inside. My lizard life was thinning into nothingness until a loud pop echoed, padlocks snapping open at once. This is when the sound stopped. Silence groped its way to the air. The contours of my limbs reemerged, carrying along their edges. Peripheral vision returned. Energy surged through me, one lost wave crashing to the shore. My body reconnected with itself, each limb rediscovering motion. I stepped forward, tail whipping, tongue flickering in sync with the wind's patterns. A return to the original state. A jolt, a surge, a spark. Emerging from absence, fading in, then solidifying, flesh wrapping around bone. The body was mine again, nothing lost. A reptile once more, yet with no translucence, no dissolution—only presence, whole and undiminished. And I crawled. And I crawled.

XII

We pressed on. Reto to my left, Loretta to my right. What had just unraveled was nothing more than a leaf snagged in the wind, a speck of dust, a gnat adrift with no destination, a footprint on wet sand. I couldn't make sense of what I felt, then why try harder? I forced myself to lock onto the endpoint, the finish line stretched thin over my suffering. To home in on the scents, I mapped a dashboard of senses, let my intentions course through them, and traced a to-do list: crawl to Mission Hill, steer toward Mission Valley, drift along the San Diego River. We kept our distance from the swarm of human feet, the turbines of bodies passing through. Honking cars jarred our perception and tested our balance. Miles rolled beneath our bellies, abrasive and fatiguing, until exhaustion forced us to seek shelter. I spotted a discarded cardboard box on the roadside. Dangling strips of adhesive tape like bloody tongues thirsting for salvation. A box abandoned to the slow crawl of decay. It looked safe and carried the face of shelter. We claimed it, made it belong. It was ours. We leaped inside and settled in. Loretta's and Reto's breathing folded into mine.

***

A memory erupted. *I am at dinner. Reto's two years old, sitting in a highchair at the head of the table. I'm at the other end, Loretta on my right. The scene fractures into a sequence of instants. I am leaning over him. His little body jerks, his tiny face blotched with panic. He's gasping, choking. I sweep my finger across the inside of his mouth, desperate to feel a piece of apple stuck in his throat. My chest tightens as I turn him over, face down across my forearm. With sharp back blows between his shoulder blades, I willed the blockage to dislodge. A cough. A gasp. The bite of apple tumbles free, followed by a mess of vomit. It splatters onto the floor. Reto's chest heaves as he cries. I stare at the mess. My hands fumble for a piece of cardboard from the counter. Leftover packaging from something we'd opened earlier. I fold it, scraping the mush of apple into a corner. I glance at Loretta. Her body is frozen, her face blank. Not fear, something else. A void. A shadow of post-partum depression that never lifted. The image flickers and it's just me at the table, alone. Anger seeps in. Resentment toward Loretta comes with its own weight. Our health insurance doesn't cover mental illness. I see myself in bed. The sounds fade into words. Broken whispers. Whose fault? Whose fault is all this?*

***

Rest stitched our energies back together, shaping clarity, then hardening it like molten metal. The memory of baby Reto choking to death sent a cascade of chills. I shrugged them off, breaking free from the past clawing at my bulging throat. It was an act of necessity, casting away what no longer belonged inside me. The cardboard had served its purpose. It was only a stop. I leaned out and threw a glance at the road, needing to ensure it hadn't slipped away, stolen from my sight. Electricity coursed down my limbs, pulling the right levers. I leaped forward. Air skimmed the top of my head. My tongue darted out, splitting scents into imaginary shelves where I archived pieces of knowledge. Odors from the city's intestines soared into my nostrils. I resumed the journey. I crawled forward, gliding over the asphalt. Loretta and Reto followed close behind. We moved as one through the city. Sprawling terrain. We took paths along the freeways, flanked by scrub, cacti, and dry branches. In the most arid stretches, the threat of rattlesnakes loomed larger. The sense of peril lingered. It was embedded in the air itself. We focused on the crawl, staking our bets on the nearest path ahead. When we reached the bank of the San Diego River, it overwhelmed our senses with new scents. Water flowed from the American wombs of the Cuyamaca Mountains, pouring into Mission Bay. We battled the creeks along the banks, where slabs of concrete complicated our every maneuver. The coastland stretched into the distance, a goddess reclining across the horizon. Trash violated the landscape, marring it with putrefied material. Moldy clothes, soggy shoes, broken belt clasps, cracked glass. We maintained a steady crawl, following the river's course toward Mission Bay. My eyes fixated on the La Jolla hills and Mount Soledad.

***

The San Diego River was lifeless. We traveled the banks in eerie solitude. The ground bore no vibrations, none of the subtle signs that animals leave behind. No rustling in the brush, no fleeting shadows. Just the weight of absence. My ears registered silence. It felt as though the journey was a fabrication of my mind. Sculpting a world out of plasticine. We turned North toward Mission Bay, passing coastal stretches where green patches clung to the beaches like mothers cradling their infants. The terrain grew rugged. Steep inclines taunted our legs. Winds raged. We ducked the assault, seeking refuge. For miles, nothing got in the way. The cadence of my crawling dissolved the inner turmoil. I synced with the reptilian life until we descended the hills. That's when I felt it. A hum rising from the earth's throat. It cracked my heartbeat, pulling me into a race. I looked up and saw a kaleidoscope of butterflies sweeping toward us. The stirring of their wings dissolved into a murmur. They circled us, drawing shapes that felt deliberate. It was a meticulous choreography. Two species on a stretch of land, one crawling, one flying. My thoughts clogged. The longer they hovered above us, the more I felt trapped.

***

A lucid dream leaked. *A sharp pain drops me onto the floor. I am staring up at the ceiling in my house. It has a hole in the center. Coworkers from The Nautilus hover above, circling the hole. Then, they crash down. One by one, they spiral through the opening, fluttering like broken wings. My chest splits open, swallowing them whole. Their betrayals, their lies, the weight of everything cruel they ever did to me. It pours in, filling me. I don't move. I just lie there. The pain accumulates, layer upon layer. My chest takes everything, absorbing it until nothing remains of them in the room. The hole in the ceiling opens again. This time, I am pulled upward, drawn into it. I pass through and come out the other side.*

***

The butterflies vanished, like a cloth whose thread had been pulled hard and fast. The sky above the pines emptied out. All that remained was the stain of color imprinted on my retina. The socket of my eyes carrying the undertone. The sound of the lost wings dimmed to zero, leveling with the hum of nature. If there was a message to be deciphered, I wasn't the one to crack it. I had no knowledge, no key. I was my own riddle. All I had was the memory, unlocked and unclasped, leaking drops of a past life before sealing itself shut again. Only when my thoughts began to clear did I drag myself out of the mental prison I had fallen into. I chased the scent of home through the reserve, my claws obedient to the retraced course. When we passed the Torrey Pines Glider Point, the air thickened. Familiar pockets of wind sat around us. They pushed upward the outline of my master plan. In that moment, I resolved to recite the promise I had made to myself the day I left the human race. *If I can't live in the house I owned as a man, I will live in the backyard as a lizard.*

Part Two

XIII

Everything we had left behind in the backyard before setting off for Tijuana remained frozen in place, steeped in silence, woven into the molecular weave of time. Chairs, table, umbrella, barbecue grill, a three-seat canopy swing, a pinewood garden set from New Mexico, Reto's red bicycle, empty vases, five spare backyard tiles, two containers of all-natural garlic rabbit repellent, a twelve-pound bag of citrus soil. Each object bore the weight of its own stillness, suspended in the farewell, knowing we would return reshaped as lizards, shedding the husk of our human selves. Nothing had shifted. Everything remained in place. I had been cast out, stripped of what was mine, humiliated, and left to endure. But I had returned, slipping through the gate, entering from the backyard's right side, hugging the fence, inching toward the loquat tree. No hesitation, only forward, drawn to the one tree that had stood before the house itself. At its base, a gaping hole. A mouth of bark, toothless and wide, its lips dry with fallen leaves. A shudder ran through me, my muscles murmuring with urgency. I leapt. The motion erupted from within, flinging my fears skyward like dust in a vacuum. I didn't look back. I didn't give my gaze the chance to search for my Reto and Loretta. I knew with certainty, carved into my bones, that they had followed. Yes, they had.

***

Inside the hole, Reto's breathing flattened into a rhythm. Loretta's muscles eased as she stretched her tail atop mine, succumbing to sleep's gentle pull. I set up a mental basecamp. My pupils pulsed, each adjustment a meticulous act of observation. Synchronizing my breathing with my heartbeat, I rotated my body like the beam of a lighthouse and forged a cosmos of senses. The hollow became a cradle for my reborn existence. As a human, I had harbored polar emotions toward the tree. I despised it for luring rats during its blooming season, its overripe fruit strewn across the grass like corpses ravaged by scavengers. Yet, I treasured it as the backdrop of every family photo, Reto's height measured in the quiet tally of years, hairstyles shifting, clothes renewing, smiles evolving. Two wrinkles on my forehead, then three, then four. Was that a white hair? Loretta's arm forever vanishing into the tangle of branches. Now, within its core, I uncovered a realm of dappled light and shifting shadows. Every glance brought a cascade of memories. Everything moved with the fluidity of the wind skimming over my head. I wondered if this was a gift for my own tribulations, a reward for having endured a genetic change. The hollow trunk, spiraling upward, revealed a hidden world of life. Insects thrived here, their movements a hymn to survival. Ants marched in disciplined lines, their glossy bodies reflecting the filtered light as they tended their larvae in intricate chambers. Woodlice huddled in armored clusters, spiders spun meticulous webs, and crickets chirped faintly, harmonizing with our breaths. This symphony of life resonated through the hollowness, each creature an essential note in the melody. Was it the perspective granted by metamorphosis that unveiled the tree's secret? Size had adapted to my reptilian anatomy, while time had birthed doubts, propelling my senses through canyons of thoughts, where I encountered barriers of question marks, their hooks latching onto my mind. Despite the tumult, a primal sensation coursed through me, spreading along the arteries that fed my body. It was gratitude for survival, for not having been crushed, mauled, or torn apart. Not yet. From the sanctuary of the hole, the brutal laws of animal life were magnified. I swung between the dread of emerging from the hollowness and the cruelty waiting beyond it. My legs responded before my mind caught up.

***

My body weight shifted upright, a coiled spring ready to release. Droplets of saliva trailed behind me as I flew, a thin ribbon of panic slicing through midair, until gravity reclaimed me. I struck the grass, breathless but intact, alive within the confines of a world that seemed both alien and familiar. The towering leaves were verdant skyscrapers, swaying in a choreography of bending motions. Below, the roots and patches of dirt formed a labyrinth of secret passages. A physical urge overtook me, compelling me to crawl every inch of the backyard. Loretta and Reto remained inside the hole, sprawled in sleep. I, instead, was a mass of euphoric nerves. My tongue absorbed the air, layering scents like pages in a book, each unlocking memories of my past life. But the backyard was not as I remembered. Where were the hummingbirds that once streaked across the sky, darting to the feeder on the house's side? Where was the brown rabbit and the mice, sprinting along the fence in relentless marathons of hunger? Where were the bees whose buzzing scratched the quiet of my mornings? Where were the dragonflies and the ladybugs, specks of color knitted into the tissues of my afternoons? And where were the lizards? I felt wan. The more I crawled toward the center of the backyard, the less I advanced. My legs trembled, refusing the command of a simple stride. Everything dulled and stagnated. Blades of grass and squares of dirt encased me beneath a sky that pressed down on me like a pestle in a mortar. I was caught in a dead-end moment. A fragment of life stalled. The paralysis felt external, as though imposed by a force beyond my body's mechanisms. Abducted yet still able to perceive.

***

A rapid shift. My eyes rotated, my weight recalibrated, and the rhythm of motion was restored. It wasn't mine to command. A force I could neither see nor comprehend seized my body. I tried to resist, to continue my exploration of the backyard, but a warning, primal and overwhelming, surged through me. I resumed the crawl, every movement dictated by an unseen presence that pushed me forward. My tongue cleaved the air, slicing the path that led back to the loquat tree. The grass blurred into a green haze. I pulsed with a vitality that felt borrowed, not earned. I was being engineered into a compulsion to return to the loquat tree. When I leaped into it, I pierced through the foliage and settled into a ridge. Strength returned to me. Loretta stirred. He pupils widened, her claws stretched, her tail twitched, triggering her limbs to ripple with life. Reto blinked against the filtered light. His breaths swelled and fell, his tongue flicked, his claws flexed, his tail balanced. The sky flashed red.

XIV

He was a lizard like us. Nature had sculpted him from the same mold, without allowing a single "why" to meddle with its "how." He was our living replica, carrying the same blend of odors on his skin, written in his DNA. He was our size, neither larger nor smaller, though slightly bigger than Reto. But Reto was still young, and the mold had accounted for that, calibrating the proportions. He had appeared from nowhere, his emergence stirring in me the image of a pop-up book. He had materialized from the tree cavity. His arrival had been that swift. He stood poised, claws gripping. It felt as though he had always been there. His presence grew roots in me, etching itself like an ancient truth. Every ounce of his immobility poured vibrations into the electric hum of my senses. When he began to crawl toward me, it was like a pianist's hand gliding over the keys. As he drew nearer, he flattened his body against a protrusion of the trunk, his head pivoting inside a pocket of air. I reacted, my gaze narrowing, muscles tensing. Fear didn't arrive, only alertness. Recognition unfurled. His movements were deliberate yet subtle: the flick of his tongue tasting the air, the rhythmic bobbing of his head. Sunlight dappled his scales, their reflections choreographing a holy dance. An invisible thread tethered him to me, pulling us closer. Our bodies synchronized with a peculiar harmony, our breaths threading through the same shared windpipe. My posture softened, in kinship. He extended his front leg, placing it on the tip of my tail. Our bodies touched. I felt the pulse of his breathing, finding his heartbeat a perfect echo of my own. He curled his tail over mine. Rotating my eye like a periscope, I studied his legs, their skin wrapping around his claws with a boot-like snugness. Thick and defined. His bearing carried a regal weight. It stirred memories of high school, when I had read about Caligula, the "little boot" Emperor. Our connection liquefied my solitude. He commanded my focus. He had come to lead me toward a life I could not summon on my own. He liberated the inches of fear trapped in my throat. To me, he became Caligula from that moment forward.

***

With sharp leap, he jumped out of the tree. He was the emperor leaving his palace. In his posture, heaviness and lightness, ugliness and beauty coexisted. He turned his head with mechanical grace, emitting a hiss that echoed through the loquat tree. Sound rippled like a wave destined for the shore. He waited for me to follow, the pull between us urging my claws to release their grip. I joined him. We crawled into the backyard. Above us, hummingbirds scratched the face of the sky with their wings. He remained unaffected, his focus fixed forward, his muscular posture embodying leadership. We kept crawling, dodging ants and startling pill bugs. A butterfly flitted by, drumming the air, while a brown rabbit manifested. Was all this because of him? He moved as if he knew every inch of the backyard, every slippery patch, every hidden root, every sprinkler tube. His energy tugged at my nervous system. I followed him, time warped. Moments flickered and skipped, frames blending and reversing, gaps and voids. Our bodies undulated. He exuded confidence. With razor-sharp agility, he turned and headed toward the house. My house. My blood took adrenaline on a tour through the veins. We came underneath the kitchen window, right across from the loquat tree, nestled on the opposite side of the yard. It began with no warning.

***

A fragment of memory, coated in hallucination, sunk into my skull. *Loretta and I stand at the kitchen sink the night before leaving for Tijuana. Our eyes travel across the garden to the loquat tree. Loretta's words pierce my eardrums, her voice carrying a bite. She washes the dishes. I dry them. We are the mechanical ritual of suburban life—parents, after dinner. My jaw is tight. Loretta's words fall to the bottom of the sink. I watch them sucked into the garbage disposal. The cycle repeats—washing, drying, words falling, garbage grinding. My voice emerges, cavernous and raw. Blood drips from my nose—one, two—until I lose count. Loretta grabs a towel and hands it to me. When I look into her eyes, I find no compassion. Words mush together, mixing with blood and mucus. It all seeps back into my throat, chopped into small bits. Loretta's hand dips into the soapy, reddish water. Details magnify, then fade to white.*

***

I bobbed my head, driven by urges thrumming beneath my belly. The memory thread unraveled from the hallucination. Caligula hissed from his depths. He signaled for me to go back to the loquat tree. He stood there, unflinching, expecting me to take the first step on my own, not to follow but to lead the way. I crawled into a patch of grass, still stung by reliving a decayed, rotten time from my past life. The slowness in my limbs carried weight. Although the memory had faded, its peak left behind a lingering down. I looked at Caligula but found no compassion in him. My claw pushed into the ground, and I leaped forward. I gained momentum. I traversed the backyard, splitting it in the middle like a coconut shell, from the house back to the loquat tree. To crawl was all I had. When I reached the tree, Caligula was already there. He stood in front of the gaping hole, at the base of the tree. I locked eyes with him. He bobbed his head. I sprang into the hole. The air crumbled all over me, light gave way to dark. Inside the tree, Loretta and Reto rested. Their bellies pressed against moss-softened ridges. Caligula claimed his spot. His body coiled into authority. His breathing filled the space. Command. The night fell, the hollow grew darker. I flicked my tongue once, stretched my legs, and that's all I remember.

XV

Images landed on the runway of my sleep. Among them was Caligula, standing on two legs. He had preserved his reptilian features, though his stance was undeniably human. I, too, retained the features of a reptile and watched Caligula peeking from countless angles. My dream was confined to a maze of corners. A sequence of images flickered by, lacking intensity. There was stillness, laced with the eerie weight of unseen eyes. There were slow hands around my throat. Caligula's pupils were erratic. They kept slipping in and out of their sockets. Flickering signals, scrambled frequencies, electricity muttering in static bursts. I was lucid within the dream. I snagged glimpses of Loretta and Reto, dragging their silhouettes into the periphery of my eyes, until they churned and dissolved. Something clenched my attention: whenever I was awake, Caligula was too. A mirrored existence. A suffocating, closed-loop reflection. His surveillance dictated the rhythm of my sleep, punctuating my cravings, hiccups, and uncertainty. His presence pressed against mine, flickering inside my skull, cracking the illusion of peace. Peace, if it had ever existed at all.

***

Around me was a void of life. The beetles, ants, moths, and centipedes. All gone. It was a sterile, aseptic hollow, dense with emptiness. A faucet opened, spilling questions. Answers rolled in. Jagged pebbles, none smooth enough to grasp. Jitters overtook me, fear climbed my throat. My eyes blinked, an optical tango. Caligula didn't flinch. He held his posture, unwavering. Fragments of the night collapsed like concrete slabs. The moon laid down boards of light. Questions continued to fall away. No presence of animals, not a single insect. The notion that Caligula could control the environment found a place in my mind. Permanent. His gaze shifted. He stared at Reto. At the flick of his tail, Reto moved. He bobbed his head, Reto replicated. He opened his mouth, Reto mimicked. He shuddered his skin, Reto repeated. It was a duet of symmetry, an unending cycle. Even the tapping of Caligula's claws again the bark was duplicated. Not just mimicry. It was a ritual of dominance. Every move Caligula made was deliberate, each action a test of Reto's submission. Caligula's tail flicked, this time more forceful. Reto responded with a slight delay. The gap was perceptible. It was there. Caligula noted it. His next move was slower, more calculated. He emphasized control over time. Reto, struggled to keep up, his movements had become more frantic. Caligula's dominance was absolute. He stretched his limbs, claws scraping against the bark, and Reto mirrored, his smaller frame trembling. Caligula's gaze never wavered. It was a vise. Caligula led, Reto obeyed. The game continued, an oppressive dance. Caligula swayed his body, his tail slicing through the air, Reto matched the rhythm. Caligula paused, and Reto froze, waiting, anticipating the next command. I waited, perched on my ridge, claws gripping the wood, observing. Why Reto? Why not Loretta? Caligula's focus on Reto was intentional. He had chosen to assert power over my son. When I locked eyes with him, he forced sleep upon me. He was inside every breath I took.

***

My muscles tightened into stillness. The sleep phases were flat. My claws were rigid, my legs taut, my eyelids sealed shut. I coexisted with the night. Silence compressed, like a wad of chewed tobacco. My throat worked to cool my body. Frustration built conjectures, anger threaded plans. Raw emotions. After abandoning the human race in humiliation, my fate was cast in the same mold. My struggles were nullified, my journey distilled into a loop of suffering. I recentered my breath, trying to slip away from it all. It didn't work. Nothing worked. My nervous system was struck by a high voltage of angst. Caligula's display of dominance over Reto mortified me. Sleep blurred into corrosive liquids, fragments of my past life surfacing in a relentless tide. His image seared into my mind. His control was a chain, pulling my limbs apart. The old rage, the same that had driven me away from mankind, was rising again. Foam bubbling to the surface. Twisted. I flexed my claws against the bark, seeking release, but there was none. Frustration deepened. Indignation sharpened. Violence, manipulation, power—they were here too, cocooned within the lizard life.

***

Desperate for an escape, I tumbled from my perch. The air rushed past me, my fall cushioned by the underbrush and twigs below. The ground caught me, the leaves absorbing the impact. My body sprawled out, limbs searching for stability. Time paused, cradling me in the moment. Caligula was there at the bottom of the tree, waiting, his gaze locking me in place. Then, as I lay shaken by the fall, he manifested above. His presence split. One Caligula loomed atop the ridge, the other stood at the base of the tree. Two of him, severed yet seamless, fencing me in a theater of quiet dominion. I hadn't seen him leap. I hadn't seen him descend. He had slipped from my vision like a wet stone, slick and evasive, his essence slithering between perception and void. Now I was seeing him twice, projected into my own fractured reality. Or was it reality at all? When I looked up, the ridge-bound Caligula remained motionless, untouched by gravity's pull. Yet when my gaze leveled, I found him wrapped in his cold-blooded brilliance. My mind spun, turning into a wheel jammed with contradictions. Like every warped, chemical-born vision that had hollowed me that night, I move without intention. I climbed back to my perch, hoisting the weight of unanswered riddles, their pressure bowing my spine. Stunned. Spent. Disassembled. A few remnants of sleep still clung to me.

XVI

The morning slid into the day, threading through the moisture that clung to the tree. Rays traveled in straight lines. I opened my eyes. Caligula was staring at me. Energy flowed from his pupils to mine, drawing me into his current, syncing me to his frequency. Life pulsed in the hollow once more. Nature awakened. Caligula leapt from his ridge, descending to the base of the tree. From there, he locked onto Reto, urging him to leave his perch. Reto jumped, Loretta and I followed. We all responded to Caligula's command, not a sliver of doubt in our movements. We recognized and accepted his authority. We were disciples, chosen to be guided, standing close and encircling each other, watching lines of breath roll into balloons. It was our first time in the backyard as a family of lizards. I took a moment, held it between my claws, and let it sink in. I had regained possession of my house. I had avenged the loss with a genetic leap into the world of reptiles. Our new life had sprouted from the loquat tree—the first to take root in our backyard, a symbol of unity, intertwining with our past existences. Wickers weaving destiny's basket. It was an equation of victory, broken down into the number of attempts, and the seeds of fear we had to swallowed. We were home.

***

Sun found me with eyes wide open, throat bulging, flat on the ground. The colors burst in hundreds of micro-explosions of pigment. The wind's legs ran through the leaves.

Joy was laid on the tip of a brush, and I was in every stroke. We crawled in formation: Caligula in front, I behind him, with Loretta and Reto in the third row. The air was thick with triumph, stretching across the backyard like a steel beam. It was our foundation. Possibilities detonated around us. I had emptied our destinies of misery, repacked them, and regenerated to reclaim what was ours. I propelled my legs forward, gathering heaps of gratitude. The backyard was now a place of serenity. Its perimeter carried meaning, standing as a testament to the struggles we had overcome. During that morning crawl, I realized that what had happened the night before with Reto, his submission to Caligula, Caligula's display of power, had receded like a gumline. Joy was showing its teeth. It bit me. The anger had vaporized, dripping condensation along the walls of my skull. Peace traveled inward. Caligula had manufactured the moment. A batch of images settled in my lungs, initiating a suffocating pulse, but I was quick to push them aside. No more soul bruising. No spears to my dignity. No shame weighing on my shoulders. The pace of my crawling blended with the grass.

***

We were headed toward a section of the backyard I hadn't explored yet. An old memory, like a fibrous sheet, began to protrude. My tongue reacted. I tasted the pygmy palms leaning by the house. The memory hooked sensors to the image, but it quickly dissipated, setting off a fire of colors that invaded my eyes. A shell of silence followed, settling atop my brain. I turned to look at Reto, my lizard son, to see if he had felt anything. His posture remained steady, unaltered. I folded my wondering and set it aside. Yet, the padlock of curiosity needed unlocking. Questions had been flowing through me ever since I returned to the house as a lizard. I didn't want to dwell on them anymore. So, I made the decision to follow my instincts. Breaking away from the group, I bent my trajectory and turned, crawling back to the part of the house where the kitchen window was. I needed to be certain, no one else was living there. I had to see with my own eyes that no humans had taken possession of my property. I craved the sight of its emptiness. I longed for desolation and abandonment. I couldn't bear the thought of repopulated rooms, of another family moving in. After my home slipped into foreclosure, repossession was inevitable. But if that happened, they would find us everywhere in the backyard, oblivious to who we once were, newly born lizards, crawling at their feet, feasting on their crumbs, weaving through their grass, claiming the land as our own. Yes, I had devised the perfect plan, sealing my fate to the house. We had metamorphosed into the unseen presence.

***

I began ascending the exterior wall of the house with a flick of the tail, daring to defy gravity. I focused on reaching the window frame. My claws gripped the rough surface, each breath playing notes of encouragement. Every step sank into the crevices of the stucco. My body bent. Millennia of evolutionary refinement were embedded in the climb. The legacy of every lizard that had ever existed preceded me. I kept tilting my head to check my progress, each inch conquered solidifying into bricks of confidence. A resurgence of energy coursed through my muscles, felt with every patch of the wall I gripped underfoot. The law of gravity, the vertical climb, the view from above—these elements combined to elevate my physical ability. I was proving to myself what I was capable of. I climbed as if I had done it before, each movement inscribed in the parchment of my DNA. I tore a page from the genetic code and executed it perfectly. Then, with a final push, I reached the window frame. Stretching my neck, I peered inside. I allowed my eyes to blink only once, flooding them with memories. Silent, rolling pictures sliding into a black hole. They passed quickly, like a mute herd of buffalo. I pressed my eyes to the window glass, finding abandon and stillness. No human presence. Strips of time, our past life lingering in mid-air. The kitchen had remained untouched. Peeking through the window, I built a mental map of everything in the house, recalling the actions before the actions: the commotion before departure, the distress before farewell. The last gaze thrown with human eyes and the last step taken with a human foot. I dissected my past, one fragment at a time, reconnecting feelings. When I refocused on my claws, they slid into my awareness like a blade returning to its scabbard. I clenched harder, not just with sinew but with the burden of pain, an arsenal always within reach. I pressed into them, using their bite to adjust, to brace myself for the descent. The collapse of solitude left a hollow, and from it surged a desperate instinct. I had to return to Reto and Loretta. I needed my family of lizards beside me. Lowering my gaze to the grass, I eased my front legs downward, but before the step could land, I was snared by the charged stare of Caligula. His pupils pulsed with fury, rimmed in blood, pinning me in place, perforating me. In a breath, I constructed escape routes and traversed them, propelled by alarm. Thick, black doubt coiled in my mind, tightening. Like a deluge of frigid surrender, something snapped. I was yanked downward, swallowed by the fall.

XVII

Caligula's head lifted like a crane tearing through the ceilings of vertigo. The compulsion I felt towards him was reminiscent of the force that had overtaken me when we first met. It grabbed me by the claws, released the grip, and ripped me off the wall. When I hit the concrete, it was like cracking nuts in an empty room. There was no pain, only stiffness. He had provoked the tumble and also muffled it, reaffirming who was in charge. In syncopated steps, I found myself crawling behind him again. The transition from being on the wall to being pushed down was sharp. We moved through thick grass, blending wet dirt and dry leaves into one texture. When we caught up with Loretta and Reto, I saw curiosity perched at the edges of their eyes. It rose and darted around, carrying bags of questions. We inhabited a tower built on raw instincts, prisoners in a fortress where words had no place, their slits designed to pierce through remnants of language. I grasped what it meant to be stripped of verbal expression. With our metamorphosis, we had forsaken a 200,000-year-old code, embracing a world governed by pure instinct. Entering Loretta's eyes, I navigated waters of fear, sailing to the edges of her land, circling her steadfast buoy, and anchoring my strength into her weakness. The same occurred with Reto, though my navigation felt more cautious. I wished I could tell them that everything was fine, that no one had taken our home, that its emptiness was not a loss but a triumph. We had done it. The plan had surfaced, floating before us, tangible, real. Our victory was an object, something you could reach out and touch. I wished I had the vocabulary to erect a cathedral of praise for what they had endured, to celebrate them as they deserved. But all I had was a language of head bobbing and tail flicking, wrapped in chemical signals. I used everything at my disposal, yet I felt incomplete, severed, a fraction of something I could never become. Caligula's command to follow him still hung in the air, thickening every particle, impossible to ignore. He was everywhere, and we were with him.

***

What I began to see unraveled in slow motion, each frame clinging to the next, a cinematic journey dictated by claws, guiding my gaze, demanding I witness. In the far distance, a camp of lizards sprawled across uneven terrain, shifting, stirring, alive with motion. As we approached, it grew a mouth, and from within it, a sound swelled—deep, layered, rising—while colors sharpened, vibrating up from the ground. The realization struck with a grandeur of its own. We were not the only reptiles in the backyard. The solitude I had worn like a second skin, cracked. Fractured bones. A curtain lifted, revealing a world that only existed within the corridors of my mind. The camp extended across a portion of the backyard, the one close to the RV space, spanning like a hand whose thumb and pinky stretched apart in a display of size. It was a labyrinth of micro-courses etched into the grass. Small groups of lizards performed repetitive actions. Paired in twos, they were teaching each other to detach their tails, discard them, and escape threats, all in one fluid sequence of maneuvers. It was a technique of self-preservation. The tail-chopping process was taught and learned, an exchange of instinctual behaviors. Teacher-lizards broke down each movement, highlighting the coordination between muscle tension and positioning. Each drill was meant to refine reflexes under pressure. The young lizards tasked with learning the autotomy process showed composure. I pushed a memory into focus. I didn't recall having seen anything like it in my past life. I inched toward Caligula and sent a question into his eyes. A pocket of wind carried my intentions. He glanced at my wondering, then turned back to watch the camp's activities, his eyes choreographing the movements while unbothered by my presence. Reto flattened his blue belly over a rock beside me. I flicked my tail to share a gesture of connection, but Caligula's tail came between us. It moved like water seeping through a crack, transporting Reto under his dominion once again. I was pushed aside, forced to abandon whatever feeling I was holding in for my son, watching my action abort. Submission always came with eerie ease in Caligula's presence, and my will felt like an appendix he could remove each time I showed initiative. Caligula and Reto crawled toward the camp's entrance. Loretta stayed behind with me. When I turned to her, the veins of her curiosity ruptured. Decoding primordial instincts had become easier now that I was an animal. I could weave into their fibers, feel their textures, handle their layers. We bent our eyes toward our son. Time genuflected.

***

We watched Reto weave through the camp, ablaze. His tail sliced the air. His movements mirrored Caligula's. They were notes on a pentagram, a duet composed only for the two of them. Wonder swelled in me. I was unprepared for this. Fighting the pull of my own eyelids, I absorbed each fractured second engrave it onto my mind. I observed Reto assume a position of deference before an elder lizard, his small body aligned in an unspoken ritual. Caligula began the demonstration. The autotomy technique was broken down into digestible steps. It was a loop of gestures that gained momentum with repetition. The detachment of the tail was deconstructed, a survival mechanism laid over nature's tablecloth. Stillness was crucial, woven into the stages of the process. When the lesson ended, Caligula bobbed his head twice and emitted a thick hiss that traveled to us. Then he used his tail to beckon Loretta and me forward, flicking it against the ground. We crawled toward Reto and settled before him. He was the teacher now, the one who had grasped survival with a clarity we had yet to master. His wisdom, young but sharpened, had been acquired through the ruthless efficiency of adaptation. As I mirrored his movements, translating them into my own body, my mind slipped into the trenches of a memory. I retraced Reto's miserable years at school, raw, jagged cuts of life served without mercy. Humiliation. Bullying. Abuse. My absence. My failure. My guilt. But here, now, suffering had been transformed. This was Reto's reckoning, earned. A young reptile before his ascent, his every motion infused with power. With each precise movement, he injected pride in me. Mute words tumbled from the cliffs of my skull, collapsing into the hollow of my chest. A tide of emotion rippled through my spine in waves of electric chills.

XVIII

We stayed at the camp, watching the sun dissolve from the blue fabric of morning into the amber weave of dusk. Every maneuver Reto demonstrated, we replicated. We were caught in the spokes of instinct. Caligula had constructed a cathedral of power with no loose stones. His grip was diamantine, rarer than any control I had ever known as a man. It flirted with protection, a fortress of safety that both soothed and sickened me. It felt right. It felt wrong. A blade with no handle, cutting both ways. I caught a fistful of rays and used them to recharge. I spread my claws wide, flattened my body against the ground, and pushed up and down while watching Reto teach the other lizards. Whenever a new class would begin, his endurance was on display. As the light traveled like a highway of heat, I noticed small rectangular plots beyond the camp, along the trim of the house near the RV space. Memories stirred, flickering into scattered dots, no larger than coins. They popped up faster than I expected, with no sequential order. Electric flashes, some with sound, others without. I crafted a map of scents out of them. I edged closer to the plots, bewilderment trailing behind me like a second tail. My claws pressed forward, my head held firm. I resisted the instinct to bob, locking eyes onto Loretta. She had returned to the frame of my existence, gliding into place with the hush of something predestined. Then came Caligula, obstructing our path. We surrendered to the unavoidable. He had not crawled into view. He had appeared, birthing himself from a dimension I hadn't known existed. I realized that the plots were feeding stations, evenly spaced and fenced with rocks. Gravel and sand, dotted with short logs, served as basking spots. I scanned the surroundings, landing on a collection of dead insects scattered atop flat stones. When I extended my tongue, the feast commenced. Clamping my jaws around a centipede, I savored the rich, crunchy texture, consuming it whole, my sharp teeth making hard work of it. I picked up a beetle, chewed through the shell, and reached the softer insides. My movements were precise and unhurried, my predatory instincts in full control. Loretta's crunching filled the air, overtaking my own as her jaws snapped louder. Though I could still sense Caligula's presence nearby, the universe had shrunk, narrowing to the portion of food within my reach. It extended no further than the connection between my mouth and the prey poised to slide down my throat. This was my naked lunch. Vibrations beneath my toes hinted at the approach of other lizards. Alertness seeped into my muscles.

***

My gaze locked onto a lizard at the adjacent feeding station. There was no flicker of the singular resonance I'd felt when first encountering Caligula. Instead, the response I registered was primitive. A tenuous thread of instinct stretched outward, bridging the small distance between us. Wariness failed to ignite. There was no path of threat, just hollow behavior, movements repeated in sequences, centered around the food. The lizard kept chewing, unperturbed, while the beetle I had swallowed continued its descent into my intestines. My throat throbbed, then settled into stillness. I shifted focus once more, turning to the feeding station across from me. Reto emerged at the periphery of my vision, shadowed by Caligula. He stepped into my plot, positioning his body behind mine, perfect clearance, so close I could sense the tremors in his tail. Gasps rippling through him. Each flick carved the air, shattering molecules into a mist of scent. I held my jaw tight around the cricket's shell, grinding it down, hunger still dictating my every move. In hindsight, I had dismissed Reto's intent, tossed it aside, discarded it into the refuse bin of my distraction. The truth was, he had angled his body in a silent prelude to a forward spring. He was signaling, staking a claim on my own prey, a challenge to me, his father, the readiness to sever our bond in a heartbeat. In the space of a fractured instant, he lunged, ascending from behind, feral, blindingly fast, forcing my rear legs to recoil into the chamber of fear. It was an act of dominance. It carried traits of arrogance, a maneuver to claim the space as his own and assert power over me. Fatherhood unraveled quicker than debris caught in a whirlwind. Whatever connection we had nurtured was cast off, replaced by a struggle for rank. Caligula stood nearby. I wondered if Reto's actions were a fragment of a broader plan. Or perhaps this was the unfiltered truth of nature asserting itself. I watched Reto swallow my prey, bypassing the slow deliberation of chewing. His ferocity was a raw mastery of the hunter's mechanics. The pride I'd felt for him at the autotomy camp evaporated, leaving the sting of displacement. I was forced to crawl out of my feeding station, remissive, defeated, and humiliated. I tried to let my eyes roll over Loretta's body, but what had just unfolded with Reto seemed to have left her untouched. I crawled into her feeding station and reached for a centipede lying by her side. But as soon as I opened my mouth to take the bite, she pushed me away, ripping the pocket of air between us with a low-pitched grunt, foreign not only to my eardrums but to my perception of her. It gushed out of her intestines, while her body was tense, firm, and unruly. She hit me like a wave, a perfect imitation of the punishment I had already endured from my son. Thrown off balance, I flailed, my tail whipping back and forth, a desperate lasso of flesh and nerves struggling to regain control. The centipede, which had been destined for my throat, disappeared into Loretta's. Her chewing turned into a declaration of dominance. Each crunch came equipped with a metallic reverberance.

***

Caligula watched me struggle, his inaction tinged with judgment. When he finally moved, a hiss rose from the bulge of his throat. He crawled toward me, a storm closing in. Positioning himself above me, his rear toes clamped down on my tail. He pulled me out of the feeding station, dragging me like a mop. While staring at Loretta, I felt Caligula's force taking over my muscles. I had no resistance to offer. He maneuvered himself between us, a barrier incarnate. He began pressing into the ground, his eyes fixed on my nostrils. They pierced into me, a beam of light cutting through my snout. Fear dissolved in his presence, stripped away until obedience remained. I blinked and found myself in another feeding station, with no memory of having crawled there. My mind spiraled, replaying Loretta and Reto's aggression in loops of anger. The bond we once shared had been reduced to pulp. I forced a half-dead butterfly down my throat, its wings damp and stiff. Memories swarmed in waves. Regret crystallized. I swallowed, hoping to suppress the nauseating feelings. Caligula's unblinking pupils bore down on me. Twilight descended, an actress stepping onto the stage, commanding nature. Caligula's tail moved like a conductor's baton. Reto and Loretta complied, pliant and yielding, molding themselves into the shape of their new fate as followers. They crawled toward him, heads bowed, snouts etching trails in the dirt. I recoiled. A visceral rejection paired with a purging impulse. Legs locked in a patch of grass. Caligula advanced, a dense mass of energy, flicking through my nerves like live wires. Against the pull of my desires, I moved. If there had been a torn page from the book of fate, it would have read that I, like all the others, was to return to the loquat tree. No stray paths, no solitary wandering. The night fell, draping the world in a shroud of moisture. My anger spilled into a void of tar.

XIX

We perched on the ledges protruding from the hollow trunk of the tree. I flattened my body, stretched my muscles, breathed. Our movements were synchronized, a metronome of actions. Caligula's eyes left the harbor of their sockets, a ship lifting anchor in the middle of the night. Darkness thickened shadows, moonlight sculpted silhouettes. Loretta and Reto faded from my sight. It was Caligula and me, once more. Our pupils darted like two prizefighters cutting the ring. Silence flushed away the debris of the day. Quietness lined its bricks and muted the world outside. Caligula closed his eyes, I closed mine. Pressure over my eyelids brought sharp pain. I found myself in the middle of a land of noise. I remained still. Heavy thumping, accompanied by breathing tones. When my senses came to the rescue, I assigned an image to the sonic chaos: a colony of rats had begun to swarm the loquat tree. Their rapid steps created a perverse sequence of swirls. Their tails whipped the trunk, their squeaks multiplied in the air. Looping percussive shots. The chewing pierced my eardrums. The scurrying pushed my fear forward, trampling the silence with a river of bodies. I twitched, my tongue lashed out, odor overwhelmed. I turned to Loretta and Reto, then craned toward Caligula. Was this a figment of my imagination? The noise didn't wake him up. Nobody was awake but me. Eyes wide open, marble-like stillness. The rats raced around the tree, finding new paths, breaking branches, destroying foliage. An orchestra devoted to

anxiety. Memories unlocked, sprinting through my brain, syncing with the rodents' race. They formed a scaffold of micro-events. Each landed with a timestamp that marked my last year on earth as a human being. The visual sequence rolled through what had unfolded between me and the Bonvisa family. It stretched from the day I brought them aboard as investors at The Nautilus to the collapse of the cell-cultured fish market. I had succumbed to their threats. Pain sharpened. Disgust resurfaced. A life besieged by loan sharks was the sediment of the memory. A smell carrying metallic tones fixed in my nostrils. I attempted to jump off the ridge but crawled into a hallucinatory state.

***

A string of code sat in the middle of a cluster of glowing particles. It looked like this:

```
class MemoryStructure:
 def __init__(self, visual_data, auditory_data,
emotional_context, timestamp, metadata):
  self.visual_data = visual_data
  self.auditory_data = auditory_data
  self.emotional_context = emotional_context
  self.timestamp = timestamp
  self.metadata = metadata

def StoreMemory():
 memory = MemoryStructure(
  visual_data=VisualData,
  auditory_data=AuditoryData,
  emotional_context=EmotionalContext,
  timestamp=Timestamp,
  metadata=Metadata
```

)

Bonvisa(memory)

I sprouted legs and began crawling into the string, weaving through three-dimensional symbols, brushing against a texture unlike anything I had ever encountered. Dazed, I jolted at the sight of what could only be called The Face. It was a composite of human features, a collection of the world's traits condensed into a single shape. The Face's eyes tightened around me, a strangling torque, pressure coiling inward, everything locked into a chain. I shrank, reduced to a speck. The red tip of a laser danced across The Face. It expanded, morphing into a mouth with a life of its own. Universes of teeth, upper and lower lips floating in zero gravity, then collapsing into themselves, only to regenerate anew. It all lasted for a sliver of time, until what was, wasn't anymore. What I had seen could no longer be seen. The Face had vanished. I was thrust back into my lizard dimension.

***

When I turned to Caligula, I found a heavily breathing fossil. His reptilian essence seemed to have drained from its shell. I shattered through a pocket of air, my legs latching onto a balloon of energy. When I landed, I tilted my head upward, stretching my neck. Terror kept shifting through me. The only escape was to climb back to my ridge, from there to crawl toward Caligula, to see for myself, to reach out, to touch the statue of terror he had become. I wanted to coil my tail around his, grasping for something solid, something real, anything to unravel the hallucinatory state. My ascent ruptured a shell of moisture. I tried to amplify the noise by quickening the intervals between each breath, giving my claws the freedom to wreak havoc. Not a single brick of time disturbed Caligula's stillness. When I climbed the last portion of the bark, there he was, just a few pockets of darkness away from me. The scales of his skin glimmered, his tail meandered, creating geometry in the laboratory of Nature. His pupils locked in inaction. His eyelids gave his nose a galaxy of wrinkles. I found a protuberance to secure my limbs. I put my left leg forward, lifting it into the air to gain momentum. A simple touch was all I needed. When I connected with him, the rat noise ceased. The world returned to silence like a soldier coming home from war. The rodent pandemonium steamed the timeline of my memory. It vaporized. All was unplugged. Caligula's eyes dilated. Moonlight drilled an opening into the tree. A sibilance traveled to me like an arrow piercing through the air. I turned and noticed Loretta had descended to the bottom of the tree. I lunged downward, fearing Caligula might go after her. My claws knitted into a ball. But instead of springing forward, I moved backward. My actions had been rebuilt, my intentions rewritten, my momentum remolded. Was all of this for his amusement? Instincts had gone blind. My magnetoreceptions were dancers with broken ankles. Body functions deactivated. Spatial awareness vanished. It felt as if the earth had been dismantled and reassembled while I was elsewhere. In Caligula's presence, I was a lizard of pre-programmed intentions. Any deviation from his defined path was met with redirection. The earth had lost its magnetic field. No vibrations reached my belly. I was swamped in a controlled void. Anger simmered within me. Loretta had returned to her ridge—had her actions been redirected too? The placement of our bodies rebuilt the scaffold of the familiar scene. Everything had reverted to its previous state, as it was before the rats surrounded the loquat tree. The night continued its work, transfixed by a liquid moon. Caligula pressed his claws into the ledge, raised his upper body, and stretched his neck. These maneuvers unfolded in a chip of time, yet they spoke with the lips of eternity. I found myself wandering through Caligula's eyes. If there was a divider separating two streams of energy, good and bad, I was crawling along its edge. Roads of dots connected backward. I had named him "Caligula," the little boot, the devilish Emperor, as if my brain had dipped into the future. I remained entangled in this skein of my own thought for the rest of the night.

Part Three

XX

Time ebbed and flowed with the rolling call of dusks and dawns. Life in the backyard carved its own path, an unceasing current, each ripple distinct, never to be repeated. We were steeped in revelations. On days when the sun hid behind bruised clouds, even the faintest drop of rain was an experience to be devoured. My ability to summon memories had sharpened, a reflex etched into my being, a motion ingrained in muscle and mind. When a memory surfaced, my claws would press deeper into the earth, my shoulders and hips tightening in synchronized tension, propelling the act forward. My spine pulsed, undulating in rhythm. It was a silent conduit for the past, each image igniting the next in an unbroken chain. My technique for retrieving memories was no longer just a skill, but a bludgeon to carve through. This evolution coincided with Reto's constant presence at the autotomy camp. Father and son had diverged, each following its own course, bound by the rhythm of progress. I was focused on rewiring my inner cogs into a switch I could flick at will, while Reto was busy transforming into a vessel of knowledge for other lizards. Loretta had settled into her own rhythm, weaving herself into a routine. She had become a thread and a needle stitching a newfound identity. Above all and beyond everywhere, there was Caligula. He had seeped into our lives, a guiding lubricant. The sculpting of time rested within his grasp, bound under his dominion. Because of him, we continued to repress our instincts, subservient to his leadership. Each morning, we would emerge from the loquat tree's misty walls, crawl to the autotomy camp, and settle Reto and Loretta there. Caligula wanted both to stay at the camp while he and I would explore the backyard, weaving through weeds. For each day, he had an agenda marching at the pace of his secrets. I accepted it like the sky accepts thunder.

***

It was during our backyard traversals that memory took root. It would drip into me—slow as dew slipping between scales—then ignite, flooding my cortex and launching me backward through the wreckage of my former life. No matter how far I traveled in my mind, only the backyard could summon memories with such clarity. Every scent held a story, curled in a chemical cradle. There were patches where pain arrived first. A prelude. The dam cracking before the surge. One day, my past life struck on a strip of dirt running beneath the sprinkler line. It came like a flood. The tubes burst. A sequence of see-through images. I followed the connective threads until I encountered the heated grid again. It shed light on a path. When I reached the bottom, I found myself at the mercy of an exploratory need that grew the deeper I ventured into the recollection. I looked crevices to explore, while the heated grid started hardening, releasing the molecular structure of the memory in the form of a pseudocode. This was my second time diving deep into a recollection, penetrating its algorithm, and connecting the visual ends that triggered motion. The stored information held images of the day I was summoned to the HR office at The Nautilus and handed the termination papers. It was a moment in time that marked the forming of a wave, rising high with spikes of pain, then crashing and rippling through. Agony dripped dense like tar. I crawled closer to the three-dimensional letters the pseudocode was built upon:

```
Map<String, String> details = new HashMap<>();
details.put("reason", "Nautilus");
details.put("deliverer", "HR Manager");
details.put("location", "Office Meeting Room");
details.put("document", "Termination letter");
```

My perception of what was happening split in two levels. Level 1 was my lizard life, tethered to Caligula, while Level 2 lay at the bottom of the memory, deep within the algorithm sequence. I was on Level 2 when I retrieved a fragment of the memory. *I am holding the termination letter, gripping the edge of the envelope. Loretta snatches it out of my hands, leaving a shard of paper clinging between my thumb and index finger. She walks out to the backyard. A tear carves a riverbed down her cheek. I watch her sway, heels on the patio tiles and toes brushing the leaves of grass. She's a pendulum of grief.* Shouting out of nothingness, The Face emerged once more. It ruptured through the slime of emotions, commanded attention, locking onto me. I recognized it now. I had absorbed its presence, though its features remained elusive. A shifting composite of familiarity moved into my orbits. I relived the moment I was severed from the company into which I had poured all my savings. Exiled. A slab of time dropped with three hollow thuds. My skeleton compressed. My body quivered. A gelatinous wall disintegrated, trapping me inside. Quicksand. I sank into the memory. Two chairs materialized at opposite ends of a table. The scene carried no weight, yet everything was anchored to the floor. On one side, there was me. On the other sat the HR representative of The Nautilus. Sound dimmed to a hiss. My focus latched onto the only object in the scene: the termination letter. The HR person's arm extended across the table, handing me a white rectangular envelope. The sound of her skin brushing the tabletop was autotuned. The letter dropped into my hand. My upper lip twitched. Pain surged, a tide against the brittle shoreline of my senses. My lizard eyes kept staring at my human self. I watched my head sink between my shoulders. Anger dripped from every corner of me. I was being sued for millions. The Bonvisa, the loan sharks I had brought in to raise funds, had dragged me into ruin. My face, pink flesh, betrayed it all. Downfall. I crawled through the code sequence. Pain became my atoll, its lands ruptured by fumes that churned out of my chest in bursts. Me, the lizard, crept beneath the table, trailing across my human feet. My shoes were perfectly aligned, resting within a rectangle that mirrored the envelope they had just handed me. The stillness of my human legs had blades—sharp, malignant filaments sprouting from every surface. A cyst of suffering swelled above them, then grew into the innermost layers of my lizard skin. I stalled. I found guilt. The faces of those who came to foreclose on my house manifested, perched atop bloated bellies. When a new string of memory began to unspool, it came all sliced up. Loretta's judgment ballooned. It rippled outward. Our trust had cracked, each fracture a canyon. I arched my tail. My throat gripped. Breath fled me. Bricks into my lungs, burying me at the memory's lowest depth. When Level 2 dissolved, I resurfaced like a miner from a moonless night.

***

I strained to bridge the chasm between pain and peace. Caligula laid his tail atop mine, a gesture that felt both comforting and consuming. It was a rare moment of openness, despite having wandered the memory secluded in his dominion. I orbited him, searching for respite. He remained still, breathing with a cadence. Under the spell of his command, I followed. Trailing back to the autotomy camp, I noticed a hummingbird darting across the backyard. A comma in a soliloquy. I smelled its wings. I slowed the trajectory, tracing the mechanics of its shoulder joints until I became one with it, then watched it vanish over the fence, unaware it had become the galaxy of my focus. Caligula's pace remained steady. The grass blades yielded to the curves of his body. I wondered if any predator could ever threaten him. When we arrived at the autotomy camp, Loretta burst into my sight. Caligula craned his neck, closing the space between me and her. He sent a trunk of questions into my mind, forcing me to rummage through their answers. He devoured my stare, leaving me disoriented and submissive. Loretta flattened herself near Caligula, their tails intertwining in a spiraling embrace. She arched her back as he pressed close. Her breath came soft. His undulations matched hers. The harmony was rippling. A poison-tipped arrow pierced what remained of my masculine instincts. I shifted to the side, slipping out of their line of sight. An electric spark ignited a memory, its edges tinged with the familiar burn of impotence. Solitude crept over me. It was my constrictor. It went for my throat and squeezed until I suffocated. This was not the end, only the beginning.

XXI

After Caligula's display of dominance funneled through Loretta, resentment coiled inside me. My internal organs struggled to rearrange themselves, making room for a growing burden of loathing. The weight of it drained my strength. I felt heavier, gasping for air, my tongue a broken fishnet. Hatred settled, a mass in my intestines. If I had dared to delve into it, I would have found roots spread in every direction, a garden of gloom with Caligula sitting right in the middle of it. Yet, I needed him to survive, which meant I had to endure watching my wife held as a trophy he could flaunt in front of me. Reto was unbothered, anchored by his love of teaching at the autotomy camp. His weakness had been eradicated. He sprouted confidence. Caligula gave him a chance and helped him find his calling. Every night, back at the loquat tree, Reto and Loretta would flatten their bodies on their ridge, obedient, eyes half-lidded in a trance of contentment. Symbiosis. Two lizards fused into submission. The sight of them was enough to splinter my pride. Solitude rose, enclosing me beneath the wreckage of what I once was. I found myself trapped within a labyrinth of obsessive thoughts. I was held hostage by my own anger. In my past life, I had endured a load of humiliation, but the crushing power of Caligula was a first. If I had a mirror, and I were standing stark before it, it would have reflected the image of someone I had never met.

***

I couldn't make sense of Caligula. He was skilled at avoiding patterns. Whether moving to or from the feeding stations, he constantly reversed course, inflating and deflating our sense of orientation. His routine-building wasn't arbitrary, it was calculated. It was designed to elicit the exact response he wanted from us. Like a bird skimming razor-close to the water, I dove into my instincts, extracting whatever emotion he needed to please him at any given moment. His way of command was overwhelming. I had been abused, betrayed, tossed. And now, as a lizard, all those feelings had resurfaced. It was the Oseberg ship, resurrected by the Nordic Sea. When Caligula wasn't around, I felt undone. His presence was a needle, probing beneath the skin, searching for a vein. He affected everything. My movements turned clumsy when he was gone. To shift focus away from him left me unmoored, sounds thinning, colors fading. I was the switch he lit at will. He was the conduit to my anger. The master crown cable carrying the lineage of shame through both my lives, human and reptile. I had endured a chemical metamorphosis in the hope of reclaiming what I'd lost. But the pain had only cycled back. I crumbled into pieces of hatred. Streams of rage coursed through the crevices of my brain. Watching Loretta abandon my side to perch beneath Caligula's ledge was a concubine's move. Her tail entwined with his in blind obedience, a celebrated marriage before my eyes. I ground to dust while my wife was being remolded into reverence, and my son latched onto a new father figure. I rubbed wounds with tar, seared them with a torch. The glands of my rage began sweating a plan. Breathing changed. My body prepared for a fight. Action fed my appetite for retaliation. Nerves settled into a charged state. I wanted to annihilate every loss I'd endured by sinking my teeth into Caligula's flesh. I spent long, stretched bands of time planning the attack, projecting scenarios through my parietal eye, perched on my ridge, night in and night out. The more I embraced the violence, the more it became the lifeblood sustaining me. It seeped into my intestines, threaded through my digestive system.

***

The sun marched through a new perception of myself. I had to obey Caligula's commands, mimicking his every move. Yet, beneath my discipline, killing tendencies sprouted. Each day in the backyard was a reminder of the choice I had made and the physical skills I had gained. I was docile on the surface, but inside, I pulsed with a counterstrokeing force. Caligula had scaled the pylon, severed the power lines of my family, plunged me into inferiority. It mounted to no despair. Perched on a ridge inside the bark of the loquat tree, my claws had a grip, my tail had a whip, and my tongue a flick. And I had a plan. I conceived. I concocted. I plotted. I was the surge of my own betrayal. I had grown refined instincts from the naked roots. Nothing could tether me. I was what I could have never accomplished as a man. Lodged in my skull was a new version of me. The lizard had been freed. It was about time.

XXII

I ripped through a cloth of moisture. I sprang from the perch and landed at the base of the tree. My eyes circled tiny islands of shadow. My tail, exhausted from nervous twitches, stilled anxiety, transforming itself into the helm that steered my anger. The brain journeyed through the body, rallying the muscles to arms. I slipped into a state of methodical precision. I'd rehearsed my attack so thoroughly that every maneuver was imprinted on my claws. I caught a viscous glimpse of Caligula and used a handful of fragments of time to sever the strings tethering me to memories. Silence laid a runway for my violence, while aggression accumulated in mental pouches. The scent of blood balanced on my tongue. I wanted Caligula to feel the pain that had been festering within me. I breathed in a crescendo, pushing my eyes to the brink of their sockets. A zippy glance at Loretta and Reto revealed their bodies enveloped in a comatose slumber. What remained was to scale Caligula's perch and sink my teeth into his flesh. I sliced through the air, winding around the musky particles suspended inside the loquat tree. He didn't flinch. His power lay dormant. I recognized his stillness as an invitation to attack. A clenched fist of anxiety opened in my belly, a gush of fear cut through my skin. There was no turning back. I birthed a pause that I wedged between my claws.

****

When the plan of attack reactivated itself, a memory entered my brain and fled my skull like a meteorite. I regurgitated. My throat contracted in layers of foam, and a stream of vomit cascaded to the base of the loquat tree. A yellow-green shower of stomach acids galvanized my fears. Despite cracking the nutshell of silence, none of this awakened Caligula. From glass to marble, he was stone. He was iron. An alien stench invaded my nostrils. I held my breath, and the wavy patterns of apnea carried me through. My tail directed my body. Particles of force hovered around my limbs. I propelled forward, cutting through the sac of air that sat between him and I. As my teeth sank into Caligula's leg, a sharp pain crawled over my back, transforming into a fast-throbbing torment. I regenerated the bite, applying more pressure with my jaw, squeezing him into a carnal vice. But a dent formed in my own leg, scooping out a chunk of meat. No matter how many times I bit into him, not a single mark, not even the tiniest scratch, appeared on his body. His physical form was radiant. His shine punctured my bones instead. I felt anger crashing against the jagged rocks of my frustration. Violence infiltrated me. It consumed me. I lashed out in a frenzy of bites, my jaw snapping open and closed. He remained unviolated, while my skin lacerated, and a putrefied scent lingered on my tongue. How could I explain the pain that intensified with each bite? How was it possible that he remained untouched while I was reduced to a mangled state? Despite the evidence carved into my battered body, I could not stop. My assault continued unabated, a cacophony of violence. I was caught in the chasm between a past weighed down by sorrow and a present devoured by wrath. The loquat tree transformed into a cage of despair. Every bite carved a tunnel of self-loathing. I quaked. The inside of the tree blurred into a shadow made from tar. I scanned for Loretta and Reto. I sent my eyes on a one-way expedition, a search through every crevice, where angles turned degrees timid, and found nothing—no trace. Loretta and Reto's absence flickered instead. On and off. They were. They weren't. They were. They weren't. Was Caligula the mastermind behind this? Or had I, in the spiraling rage, hallucinated it all? My claws clutched the ledge, clinging to the last splinter of stability. I had been outmaneuvered so thoroughly that wind could crumble me. Suspended between disbelief and dread, I saw what, up until that moment, I would have sworn I could never see.

***

Half of the tree disappeared. It was gone, as if an unseen hand had reached in and wiped it from existence. The void itself was proof that something that was there it had been taken. My mind wrestled with the eyes, tangled in the net of thoughts. The remaining half of the trunk stood like a monument to its own mutilation, a witness to absence. This wasn't the work of nature. It was simply a *no more* statement. The ruthless arithmetic of subtraction that had taken Loretta and Reto away from my sight. I radiated arcs of panic. Night descended into my legs. The plan of attack reversed into a counteroffensive. The sound of blood dripping from the wounds amplified, while my body turned into a megaphone broadcasting torment. I leaped off. As I landed, the crackle of foliage blossomed into an orchestra, each leaf playing its own melody. Using the tail as a stabilizer, I recalibrated my stance, after falling at an awkward angle from beneath Caligula's ridge. All the while, he had entrenched himself in my mind, setting up a base camp and thriving on my fears. My eyes sank deep into their sockets. What little strength I had left was rerouted toward a single mission: to look for my wife and son. I began to crawl, but the emptiness closed in, curling at the edges of my tongue like shards of darkness. A sound emerged, piercing through with a high-pitched tone. When I turned to see where it was coming from, I noticed the other half of the loquat tree had vanished. Caught in the blank, cyclic eyelid of time, it had been returned to nothingness. The only thing remaining within my perimeter was my house—standing sharp against the void, a silhouette crowned by a glow. My body began shutting down. Intestines rearranged like a deck of cards made from my own flesh. Head anchored to the ground. I lifted it just enough to watch the moon fade to a figment of light. My three-chambered heart pounded.

***

I crawled toward the house. Every inch forward was a reckoning with what nothingness had bestowed. What remained was steeped in desolation, sound and silence exchanged vows at the altar of decibel surging. I tried to summon a memory, to reroute my mind, but my thoughts lay dormant. My teeth pressed into my tongue, the sharp pain sliced through my breath, exhaustion thickened in my lungs. I dragged myself toward the house's outer wall, beneath the kitchen window. A web of lines surfaced at my feet, filling the limbo and replacing the missing portions of the backyard. They wove through my claws like veins, each throbbed with electricity, a surge tunneling trenches into my skin. As I peered closer, an intricate circuit revealed itself, its green luminescence pulsating. Dread swarmed my mind like helicopters in formation, questions descending in succession. I recoiled. Whatever it was that lay beneath my legs imprinted onto my chest. Energy transferred, deployed, released. Frequencies bled into one another.

XXIII

Loretta, whose heartbeat once struck in a sinusoidal rhythm, now bore the silence of life exiled to death. Her skull laid perfectly centered on a slab of cement. Her skin, so thin, seemed as if depth itself had been starved to the bone. Muscles hung limp, flaccidity claiming a weight of its own. I crawled around her body, instincts shattered, nerves crushed under the pressure of what had unfolded since the tree's collapse. The backyard had become a limbo, streaked with circuit lines, a battlefield where the world had been swallowed whole by an insatiable tongue. Panic clutched me. Numbness settled like a parasite burrowing into marrow. Weakness oozed deeper, an acid drip eroding from within. Sound bites clawed to the surface, disjointed, scattering into flickering images. They came erratic and jarring, flashing hot and cold, both sensation and hallucination. Loretta—my lizard wife. Memories of her pulsed in jagged rhythms, razor-edged slides spooling from a phantom projector, carving through my scaled skin, splitting sinew, bleeding me dry. My claws felt like they had turned inward, shredding my intestines, dragging them out slick with saliva. I was trapped in an ending. Everything around me was vanishing. In this land of subtraction, I had become a fossil within my own era.

***

My muscles tensed, primed for action, when a force yanked me toward Loretta. The moment my body brushed hers, a portion of her got erased, like the loquat tree, like the grass. Memories of her exhaled from me, vapor curling into a cerebral fog. I fought against the leak, imagining the bones in my skull clenched in a fist. I needed Loretta locked inside my mind, seared into my retinas. The force struck again, slamming me against what was left of her. The impact hissed. Her limbs wiped out. I was being used like an eraser. My wife's head had become a flat stain. A smudge on the concrete. I plunged into the basement of my thoughts, searching for answers, but everything my eyes had touched was marked as loss. I tried to push forward. I stalled. I let my tail guide the motion. I was held down. A cerebral thread unraveled, tugging my mind toward Reto. Where was he? Had he gone to the autotomy camp? Was he with Caligula? Questions birthed stillborn answers as a tearing sound bled into a third blow. My body slammed against Loretta's, this time wiping her away completely. The shift to nothingness had occurred. As the last part of her vanished, so did my memory of her. The cracks in my mind widened, shoving out fragments of information. I struggled to map a sequence of movements, but each step I took erased whatever was left of the grass beneath me. I looked up at the sky, something I hadn't done since unleashing the attack on Caligula. My neck strained, only to realize that it had blank spaces, crisscrossed with circuit lines, mirroring the ones under my claws. An undone stratosphere. I was engulfed in a vacuum. I pushed on my legs but found no momentum. My muscles gave up. I grew stiff. Between life and death, I was a dash in someone else's plan, manipulated into witnessing the erasure of my own world. How far could this go? The question mark hit while the cruelest of all pains caught me in full.

***

Reto's lifeless body, torn from the fabric of a barren landscape, materialized before my eyes. He laid like an empty grocery bag dropped from the trunk of a car. His tail hung limp, radiating flatness, unforgiving, final. His form curved into emptiness. Even if I could breathe life into his chest, the breath would slip away just as quickly. Memories of him as a young lizard flooded my skull, drawn into the stare of my bulging eyes, surging into my three-chambered heart, carrying baskets of love that found their place among my organs. My tongue flicked, eager to capture more of him, while I trailed loops around my son's carcass. I felt swampy, filled with loose sand. There was nothing left in me to remember. It had all been wiped away. As I looked down, the circuit lines tracing the perimeter of the house had transformed into IV tubes, carrying a bright red liquid. They squirted blood. What was flowing out was being siphoned into the exterior walls of the house. My senses fractured, spilling over into a tangled mass of raw, exposed nerves. I had become someone's laboratory animal, a malfunctioning, deteriorating reptile, struggling under the weight of a single thought: Caligula. Yes, because he had returned in my mind, thicker and wider, occupying every vacant lot. He had slipped through my cortex once more. I was to be controlled by him. Re-engineered. I was forced to crawl in circles until a brusque pivot flung me toward the base trim of the exterior wall, just beneath the kitchen window. A sliver of light seeped through a crack. My thoughts coiled around Caligula, thickening into a scab of total submission. And then, I was yanked into it. Tongue-swallowed.

XXIV

The house's wall split into multiple dimensions, each one carrying a poisoned feeling that crept into my muscles. My legs twitched. The cycle of pain had built momentum, and I was being dragged onto its wheel. I pushed deeper into the wall. I crawled into a hyper-defined grid. It resembled a cellular automaton, an infinite checkerboard where each cell existed in one of two states, "on" or "off." The binary simplicity of these states belied the complexity of their behavior, as each cell's state evolved based on the states of its neighboring cells. The grid was a shifting landscape, a system governed by rules that orchestrated the emergence of patterns. Cells flipped between states, creating an intricate dance of life and death. Layers of blocks stacked in perfect alignment, glowing in hues of blue and green, their transitions rippling outward. Each part of my body experienced a different tactile sensation. The cubic cells above, below, and behind me fluctuated, their behavior defining the ever-changing environment. This was a self-organizing system built into the wall of my house. It appeared to exist in a state of endless expansion. I kept trailing further into it. I pierced through layers whose viscosity had the density of a fistful of slime. A throbbing pain locked me in a cycle of convulsions. It shrugged my whole body into spasms. The cells never ceased pulsing. Each shift synchronized with a physical change in me. The scales of my skin flickered with the grid's oscillation. Each spasm I endured sent shockwaves through my nervous system. I began to re-metamorphose.

***

A flare, close enough to suffocate me, illuminated. It was The Face. As bright as the center of a lightning bolt, it flooded me with radiance. Now I could see every trait ever assembled in the evolutionary world, every single feature ever combined, sculpted with absolute clarity. Drawn into it, enwrapped by its presence, the manifestation lasted a second broken in half. Then the temperature plummeted. The "on" and "off" pattern of the cells accelerated, each one reproducing faster than the last. A thick pause engulfed me before noise crashed, like a load of concrete dropped from a great height. Caligula appeared. His head merged with The Face, whose contours formed an overlapping stratum. In that moment, I understood he existed at the intersection of two species—the human and the reptilian—shapeshifting through lives in a cycle of regeneration. He was pure, fluctuating energy, ever-changing yet constant, a corridor within the pyramid's all-seeing eye. He was the Nexus of knowledge. He was the autonomous agent of the universe I was in. He absorbed the light that birthed life. He was the endpoint and the beginning of every existence. Thoughts clung and clicked, unlocked padlocks. Revelation flooded in. Caligula remained silent. There were no words, only a transmission of energy. I was electrified by his presence. He coated my brain with his essence. He carved the walls of my cortex. I re-transitioned from lizard to human. My genetic map reawakened. I felt scanned with the accuracy of a blade cleaving a grain of sand. My jaws gripped. Tautness stretching past the limits of flesh. I extended, Caligula expanded.

***

The cellular automaton's grid pulsated with heat. The reflection of my reptilian body rippled in a rapid sequence. Changes in patterns were dictated by the shifting state of each cell. I watched the edges of my skeleton outgrowing the space I occupied. I was enveloped by a dewy halo that cradled me like an embryo in its placenta. Each phase of the re-metamorphosis followed the rules of the automaton. My genetic reshuffling was devoid of anxiety. Everything happened within the grid's logic. The force that had driven me into the wall now forced me to sway. At first, it was a delicate oscillation, but it quickly turned into a whirlwind where my equilibrium was recentered to human scale. I was being regenerated within a state of heightened self-awareness. Memories from my lizard life got wired into one continuous thread. Both lives, human and reptilian, fused their genetic maps, then leveled and synchronized. The perception of the physical space altered and expanded. The lizard's biological codes welded with the human information. The human gene reclaimed its dominance, starting at the micro level. The reptilian cells were triggered into a complete reprogramming. My spine curved into a human arc. The ribcage restructured into a thoracic cavity. The tail withered as gluteal muscles and hamstrings erupted, filling out my human frame. Tissues reconfigured into muscles designed for bipedal motion. The photoreceptors in my eyes recalibrated, the protruding snout shrank, jaws compacted, facial bones solidified. My tongue reshaped into an organ capable of speech. I vibrated, while my brain surged with expansion, its cerebral cortex swelling. From metabolism to respiratory function, everything re-metamorphosed. Time resumed in calendar cadence, pliable clay of mathematical conjectures. A barrage of shocks rattled me. Caligula's radiance transported itself away from the grid. Waves of shivers drilled into my bones. The cellular automaton fractured, an ever-going reconfiguration. Then I heard my heartbeat. A propulsion took hold. A torque wrenched me forward. I exited the reptilian life.

Exitus

Spat out from the wall, ejected from the womb that governs all lives. Loretta and I are back at the kitchen sink. Washing, drying. Rewound to before Tijuana. Before Geno Sculpt. Before the plan. Reto hunches, his head tilted to my shoulder. I once imagined escape. A clean cut from the human race. An incision through pain. A shedding of shame. A chance to fabricate a better version of our family bloodline. The loquat tree waits. Its bark bites at memories of me. Loretta's eyes catch mine. Dish soap drips, the sponge soaks it all. I've seen beyond. I remember the future.